*FROM THE CASE FILES OF
NANCY DREW*

THE CASE: Nancy is determined to unravel the truth behind the fiery flight and disappearance of embezzlement suspect J. Christopher Johnson.

CONTACT: George's new neighbor, Mark Rubin, *lost his job because of the case, and he wants to win it back—with Nancy's help.*

SUSPECTS: J. Christopher Johnson—*did the helicopter crash take his life, or did he take the money and run?*

Hal Slade—*did Mark's boss fire him from the detective agency for not knowing enough about the work, or for knowing too much?*

Linda Bates—*did the agency secretary set Mark up with a place to live because she felt sorry for him, or did she just plain set him up to be a fall guy?*

COMPLICATIONS: *Does lightning strike twice? Johnson vanished in the first helicopter explosion. Nancy and Mark may vanish in the next!*

Books in The Nancy Drew Files™ Series

Available from ARCHWAY Paperbacks

THE
NANCY DREW
FILES™

Case 57
INTO THIN AIR

CAROLYN KEENE

AN ARCHWAY PAPERBACK
Published by POCKET BOOKS
New York London Toronto Sydney Tokyo Singapore

AN ARCHWAY PAPERBACK *Original*

An Archway Paperback published by
POCKET BOOKS, a division of Simon & Schuster
1230 Avenue of the Americas, New York, NY 10020

ISBN: 0-671-70034-0

First Archway Paperback printing March 1991

10 9 8 7 6 5 4 3 2 1

Cover art by Tom Galasinski

Printed in the U.S.A.

IL 7+

INTO THIN AIR

Chapter

One

Nancy! Wait for us!"

Shading her blue eyes from the late-morning sun, Nancy Drew turned and peered down the street. Her two best friends, George Fayne and Bess Marvin, were running toward her from a block away.

Just by looking at their shadows on the sidewalk, it wasn't hard to tell the girls apart. Although they were cousins, Bess's curvy figure was easily distinguished from George's tall, athletic build.

By the time they caught up with Nancy, Bess was breathing hard. "Hi, Nan," Bess said, sucking in a big gulp of air. "Boy, I haven't run like that in a long time."

Nancy brushed a lock of reddish blond hair away from her face. "Hi, and what's the rush?"

"We went to your house and Hannah told us you went jogging," George said, placing her hands on her lean hips. Hannah Gruen was the Drews' housekeeper. "So we ran after you."

"I get the feeling you didn't sprint a block on a Monday morning just to say hi," Nancy said with a puzzled grin. "What's up?"

"For starters," George said, "I have a new neighbor. His name is Mark Rubin. He moved into the Bradford house a few days ago."

"Wait till you see him, Nancy," Bess put in. "He's incredibly gorgeous—but taken. He's in love with a girl at his detective agency."

George continued telling Nancy about her neighbor. "Mark's working on a big case, but it's a secret because—"

"Whoa," Nancy said, holding up a hand. "I'm lost. Mark has a detective agency?"

George shook her head. "No, it's not his. It's Crabtree and Company, a private agency in Brewster. He used to work there."

"Until he got fired," Bess threw in.

"He ran into a lot of problems on one case. In fact, it's the one he's still working on," George continued. "While we were talking, I happened to mention your name and that I knew you. He said if he could get some help from you, he might be able to crack his case and get his old job back."

"His girlfriend, too," Bess added. "She broke up with him right after he was fired."

"Want to come meet him? We promised we'd ask you," George said.

"Come on, Nan," Bess insisted before Nancy had a chance to say anything. "You've got to be a little curious."

Nancy *was* curious to know what Mark's case was about, and George's new neighbor intrigued her, too. "Okay," she said. "Let's go."

"I told you she'd come," Bess said to George. "She could never resist a story like this."

"Why did Mark move to River Heights?" Nancy asked as they jogged back to her house to pick up her car.

"His lease ran out on his apartment in Brewster, and he didn't have the money to find a new place. Linda, the girl he was going with, is the Bradford sisters' niece," George explained. "She arranged for him to rent their top-floor apartment for very little."

Though she didn't know them, Nancy had waved to the Bradford sisters many times when she'd visited George's house. In good weather the two older women were often out on their porch, sipping iced tea and saying hello to whoever passed.

"There they are now," George said, as Nancy stopped the car in front of George's house.

She got out and waved to the sisters. "Good morning!"

One of the women was sitting in a large wicker chair with a needlepoint canvas in her lap. The other was watering a planter full of flowers that sat on a wicker table at the back of the porch. Nancy noticed a thin, black wire leading from the woman's ear, down her neck to her apron pocket.

"Oh, good morning, George," the lady with the canvas said. "We just came out to enjoy the sun. Isn't it a lovely day?"

George introduced Nancy to Frances Bradford, the one doing the needlepoint. The three girls stepped up onto the porch.

"The flowers are beautiful," George said. She pointed to the planter of geraniums that the other woman was watering.

"Aren't they? Our niece Linda sent them," said Frances. She turned her head and spoke loudly to her sister. "Marie, they like the flowers."

Her back still to the others, Marie Bradford was gently moving her shoulders to an unheard beat as she continued watering the flowers. She was tall and pencil thin, a complete contrast to Frances, who was short and rather plump.

"Marie!" Frances yelled, even louder this time.

"Did you say something?" Marie turned

4

around and took the girls in with smiling àqua eyes. "Why, hello," she said. As she spoke she reached into her pocket and withdrew a portable stereo. She lifted a set of delicate earphones off her curly silver hair, dropped them around her neck, and clicked off the stereo.

"Lovely morning, isn't it?" she said, dropping the stereo back into her apron pocket.

"She loves that rock and roll music, but I can't stand it," Frances Bradford explained to the girls, with a slight note of consternation in her voice. "The radio was driving me crazy, so I finally got her one of those walking stereos for her birthday last week. Now she can't hear me or anyone else when we talk to her!"

"It's got a great sound," Marie chirped.

Bess smiled. "A belated happy birthday!"

"Thank you, Bess. I'm seventy."

"And you don't look a day over sixty-nine." Frances winked, then said to the girls, "Are you here to see Mark?"

"Yes, Nancy wants to meet him," George began.

At that moment a muffled thud came from the second floor of the house, followed by a crash.

"Well, go on up," Frances Bradford said, casting a brief, worried glance at the ceiling. "That door right next to ours leads up to his apartment. He was just bringing things in, so his door should be open."

The girls went up the stairs to the second floor. The apartment door was standing open, so George knocked on the door frame. "Hello?" she called out.

"Hi!" a male voice answered. A tall, young man with blue eyes and golden brown hair stepped out from another room, a hammer in his right hand. He gestured for them to come in, smiling warmly.

"Mark, this is Nancy Drew," George said.

"Nancy Drew," Mark repeated. "This is great." Reaching out to shake her hand, he forgot he was holding the hammer. It slipped from his fist and fell, landing on his foot.

"Youch!" he cried, making a face of exaggerated pain. "Good thing I have shoes on." He laughed and bent to pick the tool up.

"Nice to meet you, Mark," Nancy said. "Are you okay?"

"I'll live." This time he shook the hand she offered him. "It sure is good to meet you, Nancy. I've followed a lot of your cases, and I'm a fan."

Bess certainly had been right about Mark, Nancy thought. He was gorgeous! His features were strong and well defined, and his dark blue eyes were set off by his golden tan.

"George said something about a case you're working on?" Nancy began.

"Oh, yeah!" Mark ran a hand through his hair as he peered around the almost-empty room. "I guess we can pull up a few cartons to sit on," he ventured. "I do have a sofa, but it's not coming until later today."

When the girls were settled on their make-shift seats, Mark closed the door softly. Nancy watched him draw the curtains on the windows. Why all the extreme precautions? she wondered.

"It's kind of complicated," Mark began in a lowered voice.

"I'll stop you if I get lost," Nancy assured him.

Mark flashed her a grin. Then his face became intense. "I was working for a detective agency, Crabtree and Company. Have you heard of them?"

"Yes. They've got a good reputation," Nancy replied. She knew their offices were in Brewster, a small town not far from River Heights.

Mark beamed. "They are good. I considered it a real break to get a job there, right out of college. See, I majored in criminal justice.

"Anyway, at the agency I got assigned to be under Hal Slade, Crabtree's top investigator," Mark went on. "He was a tough boss, but we got along—at first. He did teach me a lot. I aced a few cases for him, but after a while, we started having problems. It was weird. The better my work got, the colder he was to me."

7

"Sounds like he was jealous," Bess concluded, leaning in to Mark.

"Oh, I wouldn't go that far," Mark said cautiously. "When the Anderson Industries case came up—"

"Anderson Industries, the real estate developer?" Nancy interrupted. The Anderson embezzlement case had been all over the papers a few weeks earlier. She had followed the story with interest.

Mark nodded. "Crabtree and Company got the case when the chief financial officer of Anderson came to us for help. Slade was assigned to the case, and he put *all* of his assistants on it, including me." Mark's voice dropped, and he lowered his eyes. "But I guess I blew it. Royally."

"I never heard about this case," Bess said, leaning forward on her carton. "Why did Anderson Industries need to hire a detective agency?"

"Someone was embezzling from them," Mark explained. "An employee, someone inside the company, was stealing from Anderson Industries by playing with the books. You know, fudging the accounting to drain money out. It added up to a million dollars." Bess looked impressed. "Yeah," Mark continued, "it was a lot of money. Whoever embezzled it set up a dummy company to bill Anderson for nonexistent supplies and services. This had gone on for several years before anybody really noticed because all the money had been transferred to the dummy company directly. It was all handled by computers."

"So it had to be someone with access to the accounts," Nancy said quickly. "What kind of security system did the computers have?"

"There were only five executives other than our client who knew the password to get into the system," Mark told her. "So it was pretty secret. Slade assigned each assistant to the five guys."

"Sounds reasonable," Nancy said.

"Yeah, but after two weeks of pretty solid work—and I can vouch for the other assistants I worked with—all five suspects came out clean as whistles. That left only one other possibility, as far as I could see—the guy who came to us with the case. Christopher Johnson, the CFO."

"CFO?" Bess asked.

"Chief financial officer," George answered offhandedly. "But why would he go to a detective agency?" she continued skeptically.

Mark turned to her. "Maybe he figured his scam was about to be uncovered, and he wanted to throw everyone off the scent.

"I told Slade about my hunch," Mark continued.

"And what did he do?" Nancy asked.

"Laughed in my face. He thought I was nuts,

9

wanting to investigate our own client. He told me to stick with the guy I was assigned to, but I didn't. Without telling Slade, I went after Johnson instead."

"What did you find?" Nancy asked.

Mark turned to her, his dark blue eyes glinting. "A paper trail," he told her. "The dummy corporation had put the embezzled money into dozens of different accounts, all of which I eventually traced back to one person."

"Johnson," George offered.

Mark nodded. "So this is my big break, right? I mean, it should have been good at least for a raise and a promotion!"

"Sure sounds like it," Nancy agreed.

"That's when everything started going wrong. With the help of the police, we started monitoring the accounts. One by one, Johnson withdrew the money from all of them—in cash."

"A million dollars in cash?" Bess cried in disbelief.

"In large bills," Mark confirmed. "A suitcase full. We knew he was getting ready to split, so we kept a tail on him at all times." He shrugged. "Maybe he knew he was being followed, but whatever it was, something went wrong. When we started to close in, Johnson was ready for us. He led us and the police to the airport, where he stole a helicopter to make his getaway."

"It blew up, right?" Nancy asked. The story of the fiery helicopter explosion had been in all the newspapers.

"Right! To smithereens. They never found his body or any of the missing money—just a few pieces of his bloody clothing were recovered."

"So what did that have to do with you?" Nancy asked Mark.

"Slade decided I was the one who had tipped Johnson off! At least he accused me of it. He gave me the heave-ho. Fired me on the spot."

"What kind of evidence did he have?" Nancy asked.

"None that he shared with me—I was just out. My whole life fell apart after that," Mark continued, gazing at the curtains. "Slade wouldn't give me a recommendation to find another job, and when I couldn't keep up my car payments, I lost my car. My apartment was too much for me, too. Then to top it off, my girlfriend, Linda Bates, broke up with me."

Mark focused on Nancy and her two friends now. "I can't give up," he said. "I have to solve the case and recover my reputation."

"Hmm. What have you done?" Nancy asked.

Mark frowned. "Not much yet. I had to get a job first—I'm working at a pizza place. But the way I figure it, Johnson must have stashed the money somewhere in River Heights. After all, it's where he ran to. I've got to find that money—that's my main priority."

"Johnson is dead, though. Who'll lead you to the money?" Nancy asked. "You can't dig up all of River Heights."

"But that's just it, Nancy," Mark said, shaking his head, his eyes narrowed. "Johnson isn't dead. I know because I saw him just the other day."

Chapter
Two

DID I HEAR YOU RIGHT?" Nancy asked.

Bess's blue eyes were round. "Johnson isn't dead? How can that be?"

"What about the helicopter crash?" George broke in.

"I know, but I tell you I saw him," Mark insisted. "He was downtown just a couple of days ago."

Nancy put up a slender hand. "Wait a minute, Mark. Could it be someone who just looked like him? Do you have any proof?"

"I do. Right here." Mark got up from his carton and walked over to a table he was using as a desk. "I like to keep everything right at my fingertips." He proudly held up a manila envelope. A sheaf of papers slid out of it onto the floor.

"Oops," Mark said, bending down to gather them up. He handed an instant photograph to Nancy, who stood to take it. She glanced at the fuzzy picture of a crowded street.

"That's him right there!" Mark said excitedly. "He's the fifth figure over from the left. He's kind of blocked by the lady with the baby carrier on her back."

Nancy scanned the photo, counting blurry heads until she came to the fifth figure. All she could see was a dark-haired man with a mustache, wearing sunglasses and a flat gray cap.

"This photo isn't very clear," she said.

George and Bess stood behind Nancy to peer at it over her shoulder.

"Which one is he?" George asked.

Nancy pointed to the half-hidden figure.

"I don't see what you're talking about," Bess said, leaning in closer.

"In front of the baby in the backpack," George told her.

"This photo wouldn't hold up as evidence, Mark," Nancy said. "That guy could be almost anyone."

"It's not just anyone, though!" Mark insisted. "It's Christopher Johnson! Here—I'll show you another picture of him. You'll see what I'm talking about!"

Mark shuffled through the file of papers until

he came to a glossy booklet. "This is the Anderson Corporation annual report. His picture is on the inside cover. Here!"

Mark held it up so Nancy, George, and Bess could see it. Nancy read the short biography under the photo. Apparently Johnson had been a graduate of an Ivy League school and served time as an officer in the navy.

"This man is blond," Bess pointed out. "The man in the other picture has dark hair and a mustache."

"Come on, Bess," Mark said huffily. "What could be easier than growing a mustache and dyeing your hair?"

"I guess," Bess said dubiously.

"I don't know, Mark," George put in. "Look at that suit, and those wire-rimmed glasses. The man in the corporate report is so business-like. The guy in the photo almost looks like a derelict."

Mark frowned. "Of course. It's a great disguise for someone like Johnson—especially after all the publicity that followed the explosion."

Nancy turned away from the booklet to study Mark. "We're not saying you didn't see Johnson, just that you'll never prove it with this photo."

Mark bit his lip and stuffed the photo and the annual report back in the envelope. "Well, if the man in the crowd wasn't Johnson, why did he take off like a scared rabbit when he saw me?"

This time Nancy's interest was piqued. "I assume you went after him?"

"Sure, and I would have gotten him, too, if he hadn't run across some railroad tracks just before a freight train came by. By the time it passed, of course, he was gone." Mark flipped the folder back onto his desk. "Just my luck," he said with a touch of self-pity in his voice.

"Well, maybe your luck just changed. Nancy's here to help now," Bess said.

Mark's mouth turned up in a smile, but his deep blue eyes remained troubled. "Can you help me get Johnson?" he asked.

Nancy shook her reddish blond hair back over her shoulders. As much as she liked Mark, she wasn't going to jump into this case without giving it some thought. Most of Mark's story sounded reasonable to her, but so much of it hinged on his declaration that Johnson was still alive. From what Nancy had read about the helicopter explosion, that didn't seem very likely. She'd need more evidence than a blurry photograph to convince her.

"Let me think about it, okay, Mark?" she told him. "I'll let you know."

Mark was obviously disappointed as he walked the girls to the door. "Well, thanks for hearing me out, anyway."

"She'll help you," Nancy heard Bess whisper to Mark. "You'll see."

"Are you guys staying or coming?" Nancy asked Bess and George from the top of the stairs.

"Coming," Bess said, picking up her handbag.

"Me, too," George called. "See you, Mark."

The girls headed down the stairs. The Bradford sisters were still on the porch, Frances doing her needlepoint, and Marie sweeping, the headphones back on her ears.

"How's our new tenant getting along, girls?" Frances asked, raising her eyes from her needlepoint.

"Oh, fine," George answered with a smile.

"That's good," Frances said. "It isn't always easy for a young man on his own."

When they reached the sidewalk, George turned to Nancy. "So, what do you think, Nan?"

Nancy Drew tilted her head to one side and bit her lip. "I don't know yet. I'd like to get the facts on that helicopter explosion, to see if it was possible for anyone to have survived it. Beyond that, I'd like to know a little more about Mark. After all, I've only just met him."

"I agree." George nodded. Bess was obviously disappointed.

"Let's go get a soda. I want to make a couple of calls," Nancy suggested.

Soon the three girls were seated in a booth at a diner not far from George's.

"Order me an iced tea," Nancy told her friends. She got up and headed for the phone booth. Inserting a coin, she dialed the River Heights Police Department and asked for Chief McGinnis. The veteran chief of police had known Nancy since she was little and usually complained about the scrapes Nancy got into. Nancy didn't take his complaining seriously, and he helped her out whenever he could.

"Hello, Nancy!" McGinnis said the minute she announced herself. "What can I do for you?"

"It's about the embezzlement case at Anderson Industries and the helicopter that exploded," Nancy began. "I was wondering what you could tell me about it."

"Nothing that hasn't been in the news already," the chief replied. "I saw the chopper blow apart with my own eyes."

"What about the stolen money?" Nancy asked. "Was any of it found in the wreckage?"

"Nope, but I have to tell you, there wasn't much of anything left after that explosion," the chief added.

"Is it possible that the money was never on board the chopper?" Nancy asked.

Chief McGinnis paused a moment before answering. "Anything's possible. But proba-

18

ble? That's something else. Johnson spent almost three years embezzling that money, and he came up with a very clever scheme to do it. Why would he make his getaway without taking it with him? No, if you ask me, the money was burned up."

McGinnis's explanation made more sense to Nancy than Mark's story. "That's all I wanted to know, chief. Thanks for talking to me."

"Always a pleasure," the chief said with a chuckle. "If I know you, you're on the trail of a mystery, but I think the Anderson case is dead in the water. That's the way it goes sometimes, Nancy. We just can't catch all the bad guys. At least Johnson didn't get away with it."

"Not the way he intended," Nancy replied.

After talking to Chief McGinnis, Nancy phoned directory assistance in Brewster to ask for the number of Crabtree and Company Detective Agency. She knew that her call to the agency was going to be difficult. There was a bluff that she had used in some of her other cases that would probably work, though, if she played it just right. She paused before dialing, thinking of what to say.

"Crabtree," said a sour female voice. "How may we help you?"

"Hal Slade, please," Nancy said.

"One moment and I'll connect you to his secretary."

There was a click. Nancy was on hold. Soon another voice came over the wire.

"Mr. Slade's office." Again it was a woman. "He's not in right now. Can I help you?"

"I'm with Fayne and Marvin Investigations in River Heights," Nancy said, making up the name of a detective agency. "We're considering hiring a Mr. Mark Rubin as an associate, and he listed Crabtree and Company as his last employer."

"You mean, you want a recommendation?" The secretary sounded startled.

"Yes," Nancy went on. "He says he had some success at your firm."

"He does?" The woman on the other end of the line sounded increasingly uncomfortable. "Well, I guess he did. He's very hardworking. He put in tons of overtime when he was here."

Clearly Slade's secretary was trying to put a positive face on things. Nancy decided to push harder. "He told us he solved a few cases for you, including the Anderson case," she said.

"Oh." The secretary sighed. "I don't know what to say. I like Mark, and I hate to ruin his chances of getting another job, but I honestly don't think that detective work is the right field for him. He doesn't handle stress very well."

"Oh? Why do you say that?"

"I guess I'd say Mark is—well, unstable."

"What do you mean?" Nancy asked.

"Well, he gets fixated on things and he won't

listen to reason. Like the Anderson case, for example. The perpetrator is dead. The police have closed the case and so has our firm. But apparently Mark doesn't think so, and now he's out chasing ghosts. I probably shouldn't say this, but I think he needs a long rest."

"I see," Nancy responded. "Thanks for speaking with me. Who am I talking to, by the way?"

"Linda Bates. I'm Mr. Slade's secretary. Perhaps it's best if you speak to Mr. Slade when he gets back to the office. Would you like to leave your number so he can phone you?"

"That won't be necessary," Nancy said quickly. "I'll pass your comments along to my colleagues. If we feel the need, we'll be in touch with Mr. Slade."

She quickly said goodbye and hung up, feeling a knot in her stomach. Linda Bates was Mark's girlfriend—at least, she had been. Therefore, Nancy reasoned, she must know him pretty well, and she didn't seem to think he was very reliable.

Nancy didn't like any of this. If Mark Rubin really was a little crazy, then he could be a pile of trouble!

Chapter

Three

NANCY REMAINED in the telephone booth for a minute, wondering what to tell George and Bess. She didn't really believe that Mark was crazy, but his story was certainly bizarre —and he *was* very intense.

Still thinking about what Linda Bates had said, Nancy slowly made her way back to the table. Bess and George looked up expectantly from glasses of cold lemonade.

"Well?" George asked. "What'd you find out?"

Nancy sighed and sat down to a glass of lemonade, too. She knew how much Bess and George liked Mark, and she hated to disappoint them. But she also knew that she had a responsibility to be honest with them.

"I'm starting to think we should forget the whole thing," she told her friends.

"What?" Bess asked in surprise.

"We shouldn't get involved," Nancy told her after taking a few sips of her drink.

"In all the time I've known you, I've never heard you say that," Bess announced indignantly.

George studied Nancy from across the table. *"Why* shouldn't we get involved?" she asked.

"From what I've heard, Mark may be a little off the wall, especially about the Anderson case. Chief McGinnis says the case is dead in the water, and he doesn't say things like that if he's not convinced."

"So you're going to tell Mark you won't help him?" George asked.

"I think it's best, George," Nancy said.

"Wait a minute," Bess piped up. "We can't let him down. Have a heart, Nan—it'll ruin his life if he can't prove he had nothing to do with Johnson."

"I feel for him, Bess," Nancy said, reaching across the table to pat her friend on the shoulder. "But we won't be doing him any favors by encouraging him to continue on a wild-goose chase."

"Nan," George said slowly, "if Mark's wrong about seeing Johnson, wouldn't the best thing be for you to prove to him that he was wrong? Wouldn't that help him let go of it?"

Nancy was taken aback. "Maybe," she said slowly. "I never thought of it that way."

"Of course, Nan!" Bess said excitedly. "You could play along with Mark for a while—you know, humor him until he realizes his investigation isn't going anywhere. Maybe someplace along the way you can help clear his name, too."

"You guys really want to rope me into this, don't you? I guess I can't say no." Nancy gave a quick smile.

"All right!" Bess shouted, almost jumping out of her seat.

"Maybe there'll be something to Mark's suspicions after all, and you might wind up solving the whole case, anyway."

Nancy couldn't help smiling at her friends. "Yeah, right," she said playfully. "Your helpful attitude doesn't have anything to do with Mark's good looks, now, does it?"

Bess and George both feigned innocence. Then they burst out laughing at the same time.

"Nancy, I'm sure we don't have a clue what you're talking about," said Bess with a sly grin.

They found Mark at the take-out pizza shop where he worked. He was about to make a delivery and was holding two boxed pizzas and a bag of sodas in his hands.

"You'll help? Fantastic!" he cried when Nancy talked to him. He was so excited that the boxed pizzas tumbled from his hands onto the floor and landed upside down. Mark and the girls grabbed for the pizzas and picked them up. They hustled Mark out the door into the street before his boss came out from the kitchen and caught him.

"I'm such a klutz!" Mark lamented when they were outside. "I just got so excited, I wasn't paying attention."

"The pizzas will be fine," Bess assured him. "It all gets mixed up in your stomach anyway, right?"

"They'll still taste good," George chimed in.

Mark turned to Nancy, the pizzas now far from his mind. "Hey, with your experience and my instincts, how can we lose? Imagine—Rubin and Drew, Private Eyes—" He eyed George and Bess. "Or how about, Rubin, Drew, and Associates?"

Nancy was barely able to conceal her dismay. Mark was building castles in the sky again, and she didn't like being included in his wild plans. It seemed to confirm what Linda Bates had said about her ex-boyfriend. If Nancy was going to get involved in this, she had to bring Mark down to earth.

"Let's just take this one step at a time, huh, Mark?" she suggested.

"Sure," he said, his blue eyes still flashing.

The three girls fell in step with Mark as he walked to his first stop. Checking the address he had written on the box, he slowed in front of a house.

"Wait for me here, okay?" he said. "I've got a new angle on the case I want to tell you about." Without waiting for an answer, he bounded up the steps.

"I hope the customers don't open the box before they tip him," Nancy mused.

Mark was back quickly, pocketing the dollar he'd gotten as a tip. "Okay, here it is. The solution to part of the mystery. It wasn't Johnson I saw downtown the other day!"

Bess's eyes widened. "It wasn't?"

Thank goodness, thought Nancy. Mark was coming to his senses, but her hope was banished a minute later when Mark continued to speak.

"No. Johnson had to have been killed in the helicopter explosion," he said, "so the guy I saw must have been his twin brother!"

"His what?" George raised her eyebrows. Nancy realized that George was beginning to have the same doubts about Mark that she herself had.

"Johnson's identical twin, George!" Mark continued. "Think about it. They could have been in it together, but the twin didn't know where Christopher hid the money. Now he's trying to find it." He paused to check out Nancy's reaction.

He obviously could read the doubt written

across her face, for he was suddenly less confident and much quieter. "What do you think, partner?" he asked hopefully.

"When did you find out Johnson had a twin? When you were investigating him at Crabtree?" Nancy asked.

"Well, no, but—"

"I'll tell you what, Mark," Nancy interrupted. "You continue delivering pizzas, and I'll make some phone calls to check out your theory. I'll get back to you, okay?"

"Great!" Mark exclaimed. "See you later, girls!" Flashing a grin, he ran off with the remaining box of pizza.

"Oh, boy," said Nancy when he was gone. "What have we gotten ourselves into?"

Nancy dropped Bess and George off and headed for home. Her father, Carson Drew, was home early from his law office and was talking on the phone.

Nancy and her dad were very close, probably because her mother had died when she was only three. Carson, along with a housekeeper, Hannah Gruen, had raised Nancy.

She kissed her father on the top of the head, and when he looked up and met her eyes, she flashed him a quick smile.

"When you're done, I need to use the phone, Dad," Nancy whispered.

Carson Drew nodded and went back to his

conversation. Nancy went upstairs and into her bathroom to wash up, her mind running over the day's events.

This wasn't a case she was eager to work on, but she had promised, she reminded herself. The first thing she had to do was dispose of Mark's ridiculous twin-brother theory.

In her room Nancy changed into her favorite pair of old blue jeans and a comfortable jersey. As she dressed, she pondered whether or not to just tell Mark that Johnson had no brother. No, she decided, that wouldn't be right. She had to have proof. That kind of information might be in his personnel file at Anderson Industries. But how could she get a look at it?

By the time Nancy went back downstairs, she had a plan worked out. Carson Drew was through with the phone.

"Working on a case?" her father asked.

"I think so," Nancy told him hesitantly.

Carson gave her a puzzled look, so she added, "It's complicated, Dad. I'll explain later."

With a smile and a shrug, Carson went upstairs. Nancy dialed Anderson Industries.

"Hello," Nancy said into the phone when a receptionist answered. "I'm with Drew Estate Liquidators. We're handling the estate of Christopher Johnson."

There was a short pause on the other end of the line, before the woman spoke. "Oh? How may we help you?"

"We're trying to determine whether the deceased had any siblings, any close relatives."

Within seconds, Nancy had been transferred to the personnel department, where a young man answered.

"Ma'am, Mr. Johnson had no immediate family. He never married."

"I see," Nancy said. "And there was no one else—no brothers?"

"I doubt it," the young man said. "He left his entire company life insurance policy to charity."

Nancy thanked him and put down the receiver. So much for the evil-twin theory. Now Mark Rubin would have to believe her.

Later that evening Nancy, Bess, and George met Mark after his shift. Nancy told him what she'd found out, and Mark's reaction completely surprised her.

"That means it *was* Johnson I saw!" he said as they all piled into Nancy's Mustang. Mark was in the front seat beside Nancy. "I knew it had to be him. Thanks to you I can make some real progress on this case, Nancy."

Nancy gritted her teeth. "What do you mean?" she asked, wondering if she really wanted to hear the answer to her question. "What are you going to do?"

"Simple. The obvious place to look for clues to prove Johnson's alive is at his house. I'm going to search it—even if I have to break in!"

Chapter

Four

Nancy braked to a stop. "Mark, you can't break into people's houses just like that. It's illegal," Nancy said. "And it's unethical. You should know that."

George, who was sitting in the back next to Bess, slid down in her seat. "Nancy's right."

"How unethical can it be to break into a dead man's house?" Mark shot back. "Come on, this is a little different. We're just going to look for clues. If we go now, we can be there in half an hour."

"You don't even know what you're looking for," Nancy pointed out. A car behind her honked, and she stepped on the gas. "Besides, the police have already been through the house, I'm sure."

"They might have overlooked something," Mark insisted. "Come on, Nancy."

"Sorry, Mark," Nancy said, turning onto the avenue that led to George's block.

"Let me out here, then," Mark said. "I'll take the bus to Brewster. It may not be the most glamorous way for a private investigator to travel, but it'll do."

"You're going to take a bus all the way to Brewster?" Bess asked. She sounded amazed that it was even possible.

"Come on," Nancy pleaded. "Why don't you just sleep on it?"

"Because I don't need to sleep on it," Mark said firmly. "Come with me, Nancy."

"No way." Nancy pulled the car over to let him out. Now, she decided, things had gone too far. It was time to put her foot down. In the back seat, even Bess was silent. It seemed that she had decided not to rush to Mark Rubin's defense.

"Frankly," she said to Mark, "this whole investigation seems crazy to me."

Mark's jaw was set in determination. He was silent for a moment, his hand resting on the door handle. When he spoke finally, he sounded hurt.

"I'm sorry you see it that way," he said, opening the car door. "But my reputation and future career are on the line here."

Nancy sighed and shook her head. He was

right, but she couldn't remember ever meeting anyone as persistent as Mark Rubin. "If you break into Johnson's house," she told him, "consider me off this case."

Her ultimatum got through to Mark. He turned his head to Nancy. "Am I really being a jerk about all this?"

Caught off guard by his candor, Nancy almost smiled. "Mark, you're a smart guy and probably a good detective. I admit you got a raw deal," she said slowly. Then she added, "But the answer is yes!"

For a moment Mark was silent. When he finally spoke, he said, "You know, maybe you're right." He opened the car door and put one leg out on the curb. "I'll just walk the rest of the way home and think things over."

"Thinking things over is always a good idea," Nancy agreed. "See you."

"'Bye, Mark," Bess said softly after he had gotten out of the car. George slipped out of the back seat and climbed in beside Nancy.

"Poor Mark," George commented as Nancy pulled the car away. "Do you think he'll actually try to break into Johnson's house?"

"I hope not," Nancy answered. "He could get in a lot of trouble."

"It's been two weeks since Johnson was killed," said George. "For all we know, the house is empty with a For Sale sign stuck in the front lawn."

"I have an idea!" Bess announced, leaning forward into the front seat. "What if we call up a real estate agency in Brewster? Maybe we can find out."

"Right!" George agreed. "If it's been emptied out we can tell Mark. That'll put a stop to this harebrained idea."

"Bess," Nancy said, glancing back at her friend with a smile, "you're brilliant."

"Of course I am," Bess said with a laugh. "But I learned everything from my best friends. Come on. We can call from my house."

"It's already nine-fifteen," George pointed out. "Are real estate agencies open this late?"

"Sometimes," Bess said. "Most people work during the day, so evening is when a lot of agents take clients around to look at houses."

"It's worth a try," said Nancy. She drove to the Marvins' house, where the three girls hurried inside.

"I'll call directory assistance in Brewster to get the phone number of a real estate agent," Bess said, stepping up to the telephone table in the living room. "Someone should be able to point us in the right direction."

Nancy and George flopped down on the sofa to wait. A few minutes later Bess hung up.

"Here's the number of an agency," she said, holding out a slip of paper.

"This should save Mark a lot of trouble," George observed.

"Hopefully, it'll save us all a lot of trouble," Nancy said, dialing the number. "I'd like to speak to an agent about a property that may be for sale in Brewster."

A friendly male voice answered. "I'm Rufus O'Malley. Perhaps I can help you."

Nancy made an okay sign with her hand to Bess and George. "I'm inquiring about a house owned by Christopher Johnson."

"You mean the late Christopher Johnson," corrected the agent. "What about it?"

"I'm wondering if it's for sale—I had heard that Mr. Johnson passed away."

"You're in luck, ma'am. It's just been listed," O'Malley told her. Nancy felt a flutter of excitement, and she beamed at George and Bess, who were listening intently.

O'Malley continued, "It is a beautiful property with a view of the river. Would you like to arrange a showing?"

"I'm not sure," Nancy said. "Can you tell me if the furniture is still in the house? I, uh—I heard Mr. Johnson had some nice antiques," Nancy improvised. She hoped Johnson's house wasn't one of those ultramodern places. "I was wondering if they might be sold with the house."

"Unfortunately, no. The furniture was removed before the house was turned over to us. Yes, Mr. Johnson had some nice pieces, didn't he? Lots of valuable antique chinoiserie, I'm told, with the enamel and inlay and so on. You can see it all at the auction."

Nancy caught her breath. "Auction? Of course, that's right. The contents of the house are to be auctioned off. Do you know when and where it is?" She was barely able to conceal the excitement in her voice.

"It's tomorrow night at seven, at the Brewster Auction House," O'Malley said. "Now when would you like to view the house?"

"Er—thank you," Nancy said. "You've been very helpful, but on second thought, I don't believe that house is for me."

"I have two other houses that you might—"

"I'll call for an appointment," Nancy said quickly, and hung up.

"Tell us!" Bess exclaimed. She and George could barely contain their eagerness.

"Guess what?" Nancy said, a broad smile spreading across her face. "Mark won't have to break into the house at all. There's an auction house in Brewster that's selling off all of Johnson's furniture tomorrow!" Nancy suspected it would be easy to persuade Mark to go to the auction instead.

When she called his number, however, there was no answer. "Maybe he went out for a late dinner," she said, dropping the receiver back in the cradle. "George, would you try him later? I'm kind of tired and I'd like to get home to bed. It's been a long day."

"Okay," George said. "Bess will give me a ride home later."

Bess nodded. "Of course I will."

"Talk to you tomorrow, then," Nancy said, getting up to leave.

When Nancy got home her father was reading in his study. She said both hello and good night and went up to her room. Just as she settled into bed, with thoughts of the day's events tumbling through her head, the phone on her bedside table rang.

"Hello?" Nancy said, picking it up and glancing at the clock. It was almost eleven. Who would be calling so late?

"Hi, Nan," came a familiar male voice on the other end of the line.

"Ned!" She smiled and sat up, switching on the light next to her bed.

Ned Nickerson was Nancy's steady boyfriend. Since Ned had gone off to Emerson College, though, they didn't see nearly enough of each other to suit Nancy.

"Did I call too late?" he asked.

"It's never too late to hear from you," Nancy told him. The sound of his voice banished all thoughts of Mark Rubin, Anderson Industries, Johnson, and the missing money.

"I called a couple of hours ago, and Hannah told me you were out. We had a nice chat, though."

"I was with Bess and George and this guy Mark who moved in next to George—into the Bradford house," Nancy explained. "Actually, I've gotten involved in a nonmystery."

"A nonmystery?" Ned laughed. "That doesn't sound like the Nancy Drew I know!"

She filled Ned in on Mark and the case he was working on. She concluded, "So if we can just prove to Mark that his client and the embezzled money all burned up, maybe he'll drop the case and choose a new career. Then he can get on with his life."

"Sounds like you're safe and sound, anyway," Ned teased. "That's comforting. Hey, is there any chance you can come here this weekend? We're having an impromptu party, and I'd love you to be my date."

"Oh, Ned," Nancy said mournfully. "I wish I could. I really miss you."

"Yeah?" he said. "I miss you, too."

For a moment Nancy found herself resenting the promise she'd made to help Mark. She reminded herself once again, though, that she always kept her commitments. "Ned, maybe I can wrap everything up in the next few days.

I'd love to come. Can I let you know in a day or two?"

"Sure you can," Ned replied agreeably. "I'll die if you don't make it, but I don't want that to influence you."

"Oh, Ned," Nancy murmured.

His laugh interrupted her. "Look, do what you have to do," he said warmly. "I'll be here, alive and waiting for you."

Nancy decided for the thousandth time that there wasn't a better boyfriend in the world than Ned. "I'll do what I can to get there. In the meantime, don't forget I'm crazy about you."

After they said goodbye, Nancy switched off the light and fell asleep with a smile on her lips. If she wasn't the luckiest girl in the world, she knew she came close.

With a start, Nancy opened her eyes—the telephone was ringing.

She glanced at her alarm clock. The glowing red numbers told her the time was 4:13 A.M.

She grabbed the phone and put it to her ear. "Hello?" she said sleepily. "Ned, is that you?"

"Nancy? It's me." The voice was tense and clipped. "Mark."

Nancy tried to think through the cobwebs in her brain. "Mark?"

"Mark Rubin, Nancy! Sorry to wake you. But it's an emergency. I'm in Brewster."

"Brewster?" Suddenly Nancy was wide-awake. "Mark, you didn't!"

"I'm afraid I did, Nancy," Mark said weakly. "And I got caught. I'm in the Brewster City Jail!"

Chapter

Five

Nancy blinked, staring at the face of her alarm clock. "You what?" she cried into the phone.

"I'm sorry, Nancy. I really am. Can you come over and get me out of here? Then I can fill you in on all the stupid, embarrassing details."

"I'll be right over," Nancy growled, hanging up. She tugged at her hair and mouthed a frustrated scream. In one short day Mark Rubin had definitely become more trouble than he was worth. Getting her up at four in the morning! The sun wasn't even up yet!

She went to her bathroom and splashed her face with cold water. Then she quickly dressed and scribbled a note to hang on the refrigerator so her dad and Hannah wouldn't be alarmed if they found her gone.

Tiptoeing out of the house, Nancy walked out to the driveway and got in her car. During the drive to Brewster, the sun began peeping over the eastern horizon.

It was just five when she pulled into the Brewster Police Station. Dawn was flooding the sky with rose-pink light.

"Hi. My friend Mark Rubin called to tell me he'd been arrested," Nancy told the desk sergeant, who was sipping a cup of coffee and reading through a bunch of papers.

The officer looked up. She was an attractive blond woman of about thirty-five. "Okay," she said matter-of-factly, searching down a list on a clipboard in front of her. "Yup, he's here all right. Now, what's your name?"

"Nancy Drew."

The sergeant pulled out a long form and started filling it out. Without looking up, she asked, "Do you have some identification?"

Nancy opened her handbag and took out her driver's license. She laid it on the sergeant's desk.

The woman began to copy Nancy's River Heights address from the license. Suddenly she stopped and scrutinized Nancy's face. "Say, you aren't the Nancy Drew who's the amateur detective, are you?"

Nancy smiled. "The same."

The desk sergeant was clearly impressed. "You're younger than I thought you'd be," she said. "So how did a smart girl like you get mixed up with a clown like this guy Rubin? He was breaking into a house in an expensive neighborhood, and he got stuck, half in and half out of a window. Apparently he'd been hanging there for half an hour before someone notified us."

Nancy covered her eyes with her hand in dismay. When she made eye contact with the sergeant again, she had to stifle an urge to laugh.

"I guess Mark went a little overboard. He's a private investigator, and he's on a case," she explained.

"Oh, I know all about it," the desk sergeant said. "He told us the whole story. How he saw a dead man, and how he's going to get back all the missing Anderson money. Good luck to him. As far as the rest of the world is concerned, it was all burned to cinders two weeks ago."

"What do I have to do to get him out?" Nancy asked. "I know he broke the law, but he's more a threat to himself than to society."

The sergeant pushed her chair back from the desk and laughed, long and loud. She attached the form to a second clipboard hanging on the wall beside the desk. "I guess you've done the police enough favors to earn one for yourself. Let me see what I can do for you."

She disappeared into an inner office and reappeared a minute later, a satisfied look on her face. "He's on his way," she told Nancy. "Why don't you have a seat over there." She motioned to a row of orange molded-plastic chairs in a waiting area.

Forty minutes later another police officer appeared with Mark in tow. The young man glanced quickly at Nancy, shame and embarrassment clearly apparent in his eyes.

"Sorry," Mark said weakly.

Nancy gave him a stern look and turned away without answering.

"Okay, Nancy," the desk sergeant said. She took down one of the clipboards and slung it across the counter. "Sign here and he's all yours. The house was up for sale, and one of our detectives spoke with the realtor. He wasn't too happy about being awakened this early in the morning, but since the house was empty and you're here, he won't press charges. Just try to keep Mr. Rubin out of trouble, okay?"

"I will," Nancy promised, giving Mark another cold glance before signing the form.

After she'd hustled him outside and into her car, Nancy drove out of the parking lot into early-morning commuter traffic. Mark sat in the seat beside her in stony silence. For once it seemed he was at a loss for something to say.

When they were on the highway back to River Heights, Nancy finally spoke.

"Do you want to tell me the whole story?"

Mark knew he had gone too far. "You were right when you warned me not to do it, Nancy," he admitted. "But it was the only thing that I could think to do. I was almost in when the window crashed down on me!" He sounded depressed. "I was kicking and wiggling like a fish out of water when the police found me."

Nancy couldn't suppress a smile at the image of Mark dangling in the window. Maybe it was punishment enough for his headstrong foolishness. "Well, it's over now. Just don't try another stunt like that."

A highway diner came into sight, and Nancy pulled her Mustang off the highway.

"Where are we going now?" Mark asked.

"Breakfast," Nancy replied, driving down the exit ramp and into a parking lot. "Maybe food will cheer you up a little."

While they were waiting for their breakfasts, Mark was silent. A friendly waitress placed heaping plates of hotcakes and sausage in front of them, along with two steaming cups of tea.

"What's on your mind, Mark?" Nancy asked as they dug into their food.

"I guess this puts an end to our little partnership, doesn't it," Mark said sadly. "I don't blame you. In fact, you were probably right to begin with. It probably wasn't Johnson I saw, the photo really doesn't prove anything, and the missing money was probably burned to a crisp. I would just forget this whole thing if it wasn't for my reputation."

He glanced across at Nancy, trying to smile. "I'm starting to think maybe I'm not cut out to be a detective. Maybe I need to make a career switch. I could always go back to school." He shoved a forkful of hotcakes into his mouth and began chewing.

Nancy studied the sad expression on his face. "I thought that being a detective was what you've wanted to do since high school."

"I guess it was just a daydream." Mark shrugged and looked down at his plate. "Everything I do seems to blow up in my face." He gave a little laugh. "I guess my bad luck is trying to tell me something."

"It was good luck that you met me," Nancy told him, trying to cheer him up. "After all, if you hadn't you might still be in jail."

"True." Mark sighed.

Nancy couldn't help feeling sorry for Mark. Jail had obviously been a humbling experience. Maybe it had been for the best. Still, she hated to hear anyone talk about giving up on a dream.

She stared straight into his deep blue eyes. "Mark, I'm going to help you for exactly twelve more hours."

Mark stared at her. "I don't get it. Why are you going to help me some more?"

"If you had hung around River Heights for another hour instead of breaking into Johnson's house, I could have saved you the trouble. They're auctioning off all his furniture—tonight, in Brewster."

Mark's eyes widened. Nancy's words seemed to have banished his troubled thoughts completely. "Are you serious? Nancy, I love you! This could be our big break!"

"Calm down, Mark," Nancy said in a level voice. "I still think we might be on a wild-goose chase. But we may as well check this one last possibility and see if anything turns up. The auction's at seven o'clock, and we can check out the furniture starting at six. If we don't find anything"—Nancy put down her fork and raised her hands in a sign of surrender—"then I say we give it up."

"We'll find something tonight," Mark said cheerfully, going back to his breakfast. "I'm positive of it. My instincts—oh, no!" He stopped with his fork suspended in midair. "I've got to work this afternoon. But I get off at five forty-five. We could still get to Brewster by, say, six-fifteen."

"Okay." Nancy nodded. "Maybe Bess and George will come along to help."

"Great!" Mark said. "I'll pay for your gas, Nancy, don't worry."

"I wasn't worried." Nancy smiled in spite of herself. She had to admit, Mark Rubin was a hard guy to stay angry at.

They didn't arrive at the Brewster Auction House until six-thirty, and Mark had worked himself into a state of high agitation by then.

"Only half an hour to check all this out," he lamented, staring at a warehouse-size room full of expensive furniture that had once belonged to Christopher Johnson.

"We'd better get to work, then," Nancy suggested. They strolled up and down the aisles between the pieces, glancing around them.

"What exactly are we looking for?" Bess asked.

"We don't know," Mark explained patiently, as if it were perfectly clear to him. "Something the police didn't see. Something incredibly small, or else so obvious that other people might overlook it."

"Oh" was all George could say as she continued examining the rows of antique furniture.

As she wandered through the auction, Nancy was struck by an idea. She left her friends and found the manager of the auction house in an office at the end of the hall. He was a man of about fifty with glasses and a cap covering what had to be a bald head.

"Excuse me, sir. Have many people been here to look at the furniture?" Nancy asked.

He raised his head from the papers he was examining and eyed her up and down. "Many," he said with a sarcastic edge to his voice. "Why?"

"A man with a mustache, sunglasses, and a flat cap?" Nancy prodded. "He's my uncle. We were supposed to meet him here."

The manager put his pen down and thought for a moment. "No, nobody like that. There was a very rude young lady, though. She seemed interested in that desk over there, the one that man is studying now." Going over to the office window, he gestured out at the floor.

Nancy saw Mark examining a large, antique Chinese enamel desk.

"What did she look like?" Nancy asked.

"Young, attractive, long brown hair," the manager commented, peering down at Nancy over the rims of his glasses. "She was rifling through the drawers and banging at the sides of the desk. It seemed as if she were searching for something. When I asked her to stop, she practically bit my head off."

Nancy's heart beat a little faster. Searching

for what? she wondered. It sounded as if the woman had had something specific in mind.

For the first time Nancy began to wonder if maybe Mark was on the trail of Johnson's embezzled money.

Maybe someone else was after the money, too!

Chapter

Six

H OW ODD," Nancy said, throwing the manager an understanding smile. "Did this woman say what she was after?"

The manager shook his head. "I finally asked her to go," he told Nancy. "She just wouldn't leave the desk alone, and I was afraid she would damage it."

When Nancy returned to her friends, she saw that more people had filed in, all waiting for the auction to begin. Mark was still studying the desk. She debated whether or not to mention the mysterious dark-haired woman to him, but decided against it. She didn't want to set him off unless she had a definite lead.

Mark beckoned her over and said in a cautious low voice, "This desk is a Shenzu original, Nancy. When I was a kid, I used to help out at my uncle's antique store, and he told me all about these. They're worth thousands of dollars and have all sorts of secret compartments! Each is hidden in a different way, too. Something could be in this desk, and the police would never have known about it! Look, I'll show you."

As she watched, Mark found no less than three hidden drawers. All were empty, unfortunately. Then, before they could examine the desk any further, the auctioneer banged his gavel for the sale to begin.

After registering they took seats in front of the auctioneer's podium. The hall had filled quickly, with a substantial crowd of potential bidders. Nancy glanced over the crowd, looking for a man with a mustache or a young woman with long brown hair. All the women she saw were middle-aged, though, and the two men who had mustaches didn't look like the guy in Mark's instant photo.

"I've got to have another look at that desk!" Mark whispered furiously.

"There's no more time, Mark," Nancy whispered back. "How are you going to get another look?"

"If I have to buy the desk, I'll buy it, that's all," he said in a determined voice.

"But you said yourself that type of desk is worth thousands of dollars!"

Mark shook his head. "Maybe we'll get lucky and nobody else will bid on it. Not many people know the difference between a Shenzu and an ordinary Chinese desk."

"What if the price gets too high?" Nancy demanded.

Mark stared at her for a second. "How much can you lend me?"

Nancy drew back. "Forget it! I've helped as much as I can, but this is asking too much. I mean—"

"Nancy," Mark interrupted, "we can always resell it! Consider it as an investment!"

Nancy sighed. Well, she told herself, I *could* resell it. And also, I do think it's worth trying to find out what that woman was after.

"Okay," she muttered at last.

George reached over the backs of the chairs and tapped her on the shoulder. "Hey, Nan, they're up to the desk."

Nancy came alert and so did Mark. From his podium the auctioneer said, "Now we have a lovely antique Chinese desk. The bidding will begin at one hundred dollars. Do I have a bid?"

Mark raised his hand.

"One hundred from the young gentleman over there," the auctioneer began to chant in a singsong voice. "Do I have two, two hundred dollars?"

"Two hundred!" The bid came from a little

man with glasses sitting in the row behind them.

Mark gritted his teeth. He raised his hand. "Two-fifty," he shouted.

"Four hundred," cried the little man.

"I have four hundred!" crowed the auctioneer. "Do I have five? Five hundred dollars, will you give me five?"

Mark tugged at Nancy's sleeve. "Do you have any credit cards with you?"

"Yes, but—"

"Five hundred!" Mark shouted.

"I have five hundred dollars!" the auctioneer cried. "Will I get six? Who'll bid six—"

"One thousand!" the little man cried out, waving his hand furiously.

Nancy felt herself breaking out into a cold sweat. She looked hard at the little man, carefully committing his face to memory.

"Eleven hundred!" shouted Mark, throwing a hand into the air again.

Nancy grabbed his arm. "No, Mark!" she said angrily. "No more. You're already over the limit on my credit card."

"Two thousand!" the little man called out.

There were murmurs from the audience, and it was evident that people were enjoying the bidding war.

"Mark, that's it!" Nancy warned. "No more! I'm serious."

Mark's face fell, and he slumped down in his

chair. The auctioneer called for higher bids but the room was silent.

"Two thousand once, two thousand twice . . ." The auctioneer waited briefly, then slammed his gavel down. "Sold, to the gentleman in the second row, for two thousand dollars!"

Nancy, Mark, George, and Bess filed out of the auction house and stood in the cool evening air, thinking about what had happened.

"Maybe he knew it was a genuine whatever-it-was," Bess said with a shrug.

"Shenzu," Mark said. "Maybe. But maybe not. I'm going to find out."

Just then the little man emerged from the auction house, the moonlight glinting off his glasses.

"Excuse me," Mark said, turning to the man. "Would you mind telling me why you bid so high on that desk?"

The little man recognized Mark as the person he had been bidding against.

"I'm only a designated bidder," he told them. "I'm not the new owner of the piece."

"Well, who is?" Mark pressed him.

The little man smiled. "I'm not permitted to divulge that. If you'll excuse me . . ." He brushed past Mark and walked up to a waiting van. Two husky men in dark clothes were waiting beside it. At the little man's instructions, they went inside the auction house and soon emerged carrying the heavy desk. As Mark, Nancy, George, and Bess watched, they loaded the desk into the van.

"Come on. Let's get out of here," Mark said to the girls in a louder than normal voice.

They piled into the Mustang, and Nancy drove out of the parking lot.

"Pull over!" Mark commanded. "And turn off your lights. We can wait for the van here."

Nancy smiled. This time, Mark was right on target. She had planned on doing exactly the same thing. She wanted to know where the desk was going—and to whom. It would be very interesting if the new owner turned out to be a young woman with long, dark hair.

"Oh, no." Bess sank back in her seat. "We're following them, aren't we? Oh, I hate car chases."

Just then the van pulled out of the lot. After giving it a good head start, Nancy slipped her Mustang onto the road and followed.

The van drove to the outskirts of River Heights. It turned off on a narrow road marked by a sign that read Landfill.

"Hey," mused George. "It's the dump. What do you suppose—"

"Shhh!" Mark said.

Nancy doused the lights and slowed the Mustang to a crawl as she turned off on the road to the landfill site. The van drove uphill and disappeared over the crest.

Nancy noticed a gravel road off to her left. She turned onto it. The road twisted along the slope of the hill and ended at the edge of a woodlot. Nancy stopped the car.

"Do you think they can see us?" George wondered.

"It's too dark out," Nancy said. "And we are pretty much hidden by the hill."

"Come on!" Mark urged them in a loud whisper. "Let's watch what they're doing."

They walked to the top of the hill, where they were able to look down on the landfill. Its mass seemed to stretch to the horizon, where the glow of River Heights lit the sky. The van was silhouetted at the edge of the dump in the light from the moon. Mark motioned the girls to get down. Nancy crouched beside him.

"Look," Mark whispered. "There's another car there. I thought I just saw someone get out."

Nancy peered through the darkness. Mark was right. A heavyset man of medium height was waiting beside a late-model car.

The two husky men got out of the van and had a brief conversation with the man who had been waiting for them. Nancy wished she could get closer to hear what they were saying.

At last the two men opened the back door of the van. They lifted the desk out and pushed it over on its side. It fell to the ground.

"For the price they paid, they're sure treating that desk roughly," Nancy whispered. They watched the third man hand something to the two men from the van, who then got back inside. The van's engine roared to life. It backed up, and soon disappeared down the road toward the highway.

As soon as it was gone, the lone man at the landfill site turned on a flashlight and began examining the desk.

"Obviously he must be the buyer," Nancy said. She wondered what had become of the dark-haired woman. Maybe she had merely been an overzealous antique hunter. She hadn't bothered to show up for the auction, that was certain.

"He's checking for hidden compartments!" Mark whispered.

Sure enough, the man was pulling apart the drawers and searching through them one at a time. After he scrutinized each one, he threw it aside and went back to his search.

"Can you believe this?" Mark asked Nancy.

The heavyset man went to the trunk of the car and emerged with an ax. Suddenly he began hacking the valuable antique to pieces. From time to time he would stop to search through the splinters of broken wood and smashed enamel. When he was finished, the desk was nothing but a pile of trash.

From her hillside hiding spot, Nancy watched him step back from his awful handiwork. Then he returned the ax to the trunk and came back with a large can. He started pouring something on the remains of the Chinese desk.

"It's gasoline!" Mark cried. He began to get up. "Come on, we've got to stop him!"

But before he could get any further, a match flared. Instantly the pile of splintered wood was engulfed in a ball of fire!

Chapter
Seven

Even from a distance, the glow of the blazing fire threw moving shadows across Nancy and her friends' startled faces.

Nancy grabbed Mark's arm and pulled him back. "If there was any evidence in that desk, it's gone now," she whispered.

"The only thing left will be a pile of ashes," George agreed.

"Oh, no," Mark moaned. "Finally I get a lead, and there it goes—right up in flames. Well, that's the end of it. Now I guess I go back to flinging and delivering pizzas for the rest of my life."

Nancy grabbed his shoulder. Despite the Chinese desk's fiery finish, she had learned a lot from the evening's adventure.

First and foremost, Mark Rubin—despite his goofy manner—really was onto something. She wasn't sure even Mark knew exactly what that something was. But people didn't secretly buy valuable desks at auctions, have them delivered to landfills, hack them to pieces, and set them on fire unless they were up to something—something quite illegal.

"You're not giving up, Mark," Nancy said firmly. "Not as long as I'm around."

Mark studied her. "Aren't our twelve hours almost up?" he asked. "Or are you saying you're going to stay on this with me?"

Nancy nodded slowly. "You got it, Mark. And you're wrong about the evidence going up in smoke. Whatever that guy was looking for in that desk, we all saw that he didn't find it. What I'd like to know now is who he was, what he wanted, and why."

"He's leaving," Bess called in an urgent whisper.

Nancy glanced back down at the landfill site, where the pile of splintered wood was fast turning into charred embers. The man who had set the fire had climbed back into his car and was starting onto the road that led back to the highway.

"We can follow him!" Mark said excitedly.

Nancy nodded. "Let's go!"

They raced for Nancy's car and piled in. Nancy headed back toward the main road with her lights out. She navigated slowly in the darkness.

"Hurry," Mark urged. "He'll get away!"

"I can't go any faster," Nancy cautioned. "I don't want him to see us."

They saw the red taillights of the car when they winked out and turned off the gravel side road onto the main road. Nancy followed at a considerable distance. The car approached the entrance to the highway, slowed, and turned left.

"He's heading back to Brewster," Mark said under his breath.

Nancy stepped on the gas, and moments later, she turned onto the highway. She put her lights on. The car they were following was almost half a mile away, and traveling faster than the speed limit.

"Faster!" George cried from the back seat. "He's getting away." Beside her, Bess was pale. Car chases really were one of her least favorite things in the world.

Nancy's eyes flicked down to the speedometer. The needle was rapidly approaching sixty, and still the car they were following was growing smaller in the distance. She accelerated until the Mustang was traveling just at sixty-five.

As they approached the Brewster town line, the other car slowed and Nancy began to gain on her quarry. A traffic light loomed ahead, at an intersection with a gas station on each corner. It changed from green to amber. Both cars slowed, and the distance between them lessened.

"It's a Chevy," said Mark. "Recent model."

"Can you see the license plate?" George demanded, leaning forward from the back seat.

Mark was straining against the shoulder harness, with his face almost pressed up against the windshield. He shook his head. "Uh-uh. It looks like it's covered with mud or something."

Nancy kept her eyes on the amber light, silently urging it to turn to red. It seemed to be taking forever. The Chevy was only a few hundred feet ahead and almost at the intersection.

"Don't look now," Bess said from the back seat. "But there's a police car in the lot of that service station."

The light was still amber, but the Chevy had braked to an almost complete stop. Nancy was relieved. She pressed harder on her brake pedal, and the Mustang slowed rapidly. She changed lanes, in order to pull up beside the Chevy to get a look at its driver.

Suddenly the driver of the Chevy hit the gas. The car zipped across the intersection just as the light changed from amber to red.

"No!" Mark almost shrieked. Anger distorted his face. "Go for it, Nancy. Don't let them get away!"

Nancy bit her lip. The driver must have noticed her tailing him. Should she try to follow him?

"That police car is pulling out of the service station," Bess warned. "Maybe they'll go after them for going through a red."

"I can't go," Nancy told Mark. "I'll just get a ticket if I do." She kept a steady pressure on the brake pedal and the Mustang slowed to a complete stop at the red light.

Mark slumped back in his seat. The police car pulled up to the light beside Nancy. Inside, the two officers were chatting, apparently unaware of the interrupted car chase that had just taken place in front of their eyes.

"We were so close!" Mark said, shaking his fist in the direction of the disappearing taillights. "Now what?"

Nancy gave him a tired smile. "Now we go back to River Heights and get a good night's sleep. We've got a lot to do tomorrow."

The next day at ten o'clock, Mark met Nancy at her house. Nancy had barely opened the door when the first breathless words tumbled out of his mouth.

"So what next?"

She motioned him to follow her to the

kitchen. Hannah Gruen, the Drews' house-keeper, was just putting away the breakfast dishes.

"I have some things to do in the garden," said Hannah after Nancy had introduced Mark to her. "I'll leave you two alone to talk."

After Hannah had left, Nancy got glasses out of the cupboard and set them on the counter. Mark sat on a stool. She poured them each a glass of juice.

"First," she began, finally addressing Mark's question, "we go over everything that's hap-pened. Then we decide on a plan of action."

Nancy questioned Mark for more than an hour, going over all the details of the case from beginning to end. Although Mark mentioned a few minor details she hadn't heard before, Nancy felt stymied when they had finished.

Mark was staring at her expectantly.

Nancy laughed. "You think I'm just going to come out with the solution, don't you?"

Now it was Mark's turn to laugh. "Yes," he said. "And I expect it to be brilliant, Detective Drew."

"Well, I'm sorry to disappoint you, but I'm afraid we're both going to have to mull things over for a while," Nancy told him. "What I'd like to do is go downtown. I want you to show me where you thought you saw Johnson."

"No problem," Mark said eagerly.

Twenty minutes later they were in the shopping district. Mark led her to the street where he had taken the blurry instant photograph.

"I don't really see what we're going to find out," he said. "I saw him almost a week ago."

"You never know," Nancy replied in a tone that was deliberately mysterious. She grinned and added, "Seriously, it will help me get a feel for what happened that day."

Mark came to a stop on the sidewalk and pointed in different directions. "Here's the jewelry store, there's the camera shop. That means I was here and he was over there."

Mark stood Nancy in one spot and flung himself ahead of some shoppers to demonstrate Johnson's position.

"Okay," Nancy noted. "Then where did he go?"

"I told you. He bolted," Mark said. He pointed up the street. "That way."

"And you went after him?"

"Right. Until he dashed across the railroad tracks and the train came."

"Let's do it," Nancy suggested. "Exactly what Johnson did."

"Sure." Mark sprang into action. Together, they dodged a slow-moving group of shoppers and sped toward the railroad tracks.

When they got to the tracks, Mark stopped. "The train came, and that was it. I was stuck here, where we are now. The whole thing didn't take more than two minutes." He looked at her. "So?"

"Hmmm," Nancy murmured, deep in thought. Then she looked up at Mark. "How fast was the train coming?"

Mark shrugged. "Fast. It looked as if he had to jump to clear it."

Nancy backed up and took a running start. As she reached the open railroad barrier, she imagined an enormous train engine hurtling toward her, and she leaped across the tracks.

As she did, her sunglasses bounced off her face. She kept going until she was clear of the tracks on the other side. Mark approached, walking at a more leisurely pace.

"That was it," he called. "Exactly."

Nancy pondered what they had just done, glancing all around them. The street ran into a residential neighborhood of seedy tenement buildings. The man could have gone down any street, into any building. She hated to tell Mark, but it seemed as if their efforts had been useless.

"What now?" Mark asked, waiting for more instructions from Nancy.

"Now I'm going to get my sunglasses," she said. "They fell off when I jumped across the tracks."

Mark followed her back to where she had dropped her sunglasses. They lay on the gravel bed near the metal rail.

"The guy I chased was wearing sunglasses, too," Mark said, bending down to retrieve her glasses for her.

At the moment that he spoke, Nancy spotted something glinting underneath the rail, not far from where she had jumped. She knelt and dug her hands into the gravel.

She came up with a pair of mangled sunglasses, smashed and missing their stems. They looked as if they had been run over by a train.

"Are these them?" Nancy said, dropping them into Mark's outstretched hand.

Mark looked stunned.

"Nancy, you're a genius. You found Johnson's glasses!"

Chapter

Eight

LOOK, I'LL SHOW YOU," Mark said eagerly. He dug the photo out of his jacket pocket and showed it to Nancy, holding the ruined glasses beside it. They looked like the ones worn by the man in the photo.

"Johnson's glasses," Mark repeated, gloating a little.

Nancy pursed her lips. "They may be the same glasses," she said, "but there's still no proof that the man you saw was Johnson."

"I told you, he bolted when I saw him!" Mark insisted. "That's got to prove something!"

"It could be that when you started staring at him, he got scared," she said. "I'm not trying to cut you down, Mark, but we have to go over all the angles." She thought for a minute. "Now, we do know Johnson wore glasses. He had them on in his corporate portrait."

Mark held up the sunglasses and peered through what remained of the lenses. "These do look like corrective lenses. You know, if we could get an optician to tell us what strength these lenses are, and then if we found out what Johnson's prescription was . . ."

A broad smile spread across Nancy's face. "You are a detective," she said, nodding her head.

Mark returned her smile. He pocketed the glasses. "I'll check it out."

"If they do turn out to be a match, we still have to figure out how Johnson survived a fiery helicopter explosion," Nancy pointed out.

"Why don't we go out to the airport and talk to people there?" Mark suggested. He gestured back to the railroad tracks. "Who knows? Something else might turn up that's been overlooked."

"Exactly what I was thinking," Nancy said. She glanced at her wristwatch. "It's almost noon. Let's drive out to the airfield. Maybe Bess and George can join us."

"Whatever you say," Mark replied, giving her a happy little bow as she stepped in front of him.

Nancy and Mark found George and Bess at the Marvins' house. They all piled into

Nancy's car, and twenty minutes later they arrived at the airport. The helicopter service was headquartered in a large hangar that served as a maintenance depot and storage area also. Five helicopters, in various stages of repair, were parked inside.

The manager, "Mac" MacIlvaney, was working behind a desk in a cluttered office at the rear of the hangar. MacIlvaney was a retired marine officer, tall and broad-shouldered, with short-clipped salt-and-pepper hair. Since Carson Drew occasionally used the helicopter service for business trips to nearby cities, Nancy had met him before.

"Hello!" Nancy said, knocking lightly on the door frame before entering the office with her friends.

"Why, if it isn't Nancy Drew!" MacIlvaney exclaimed. "What brings you out here? Need a helicopter?"

"Sort of," Nancy told him. "Actually, I'd like to talk to you for a minute if I could."

"Me?" Mac looked surprised, but gave Nancy a little smile. "What'd I do to rate a visit from three beautiful women?" He winked at Mark.

Nancy introduced her friends to MacIlvaney.

"Seriously, Mac," she continued, "I need to pick your brain. Remember the Anderson Industries case?"

Mac threw his arms into the air in a gesture of hopelessness. "How can I forget? I lost one of my best choppers that night."

"How did it happen, Mac? Tell me everything you remember."

MacIlvaney gave her an odd look. "You aren't nosing around on a case, are you? Your father tells me you have a habit of getting involved in some pretty strange situations."

Nancy gulped. She could never be sure if her reputation was going to work for or against her. Sometimes people didn't want to get involved in mysterious goings-on, even if they were nothing more than innocent bystanders.

"Well, I guess you could say I was checking into some loose ends involving the case," Nancy said carefully. "I have read all the newspaper accounts, but the facts are always better from the horse's mouth."

"I know how proud your dad is of you, so it would be a pleasure to help Carson Drew's daughter." MacIlvaney slammed his account books shut and pushed his chair back from the desk to give her his undivided attention.

"I had the chopper out on the runway, ready to fuel up that night," he began. "I was going to Chicago. I went into the office to make a quick call. The next thing I know was that my chopper was hovering over the landing pad, and police cars were swarming all over the runways. Johnson must have known how to fly a chopper because it isn't something you pick up by looking at the instrument panel."

"He was a naval pilot," Mark volunteered. "I found that out when I was checking him out at Crabtree."

Nancy nodded. She remembered reading it in his bio in the corporate report, too.

"Yeah, well, that explains that part of it," Mac murmured. "So there I was, standing on the landing pad, watching my best helicopter fly off without me, and a herd of police cars chasing down the runways after it. Next thing I know, it's about a mile away, coming down low over Hoffner's farm out beyond the airport limits. Then suddenly it blows up."

He reached toward a basket filled with papers on one side of his desk and flicked a pile of forms. "Since then, it's been one insurance form after another," he finished sadly. Then he shook his head.

"You know," he added, "what I still don't understand is why the helicopter blew up like that."

"What do you mean?" Nancy asked, puzzled. "According to the news reports, when the police fired at it they hit the fuel tank."

Mac ran his hand over his crew cut and scratched the back of his head. "That's a good explanation, Nancy, but remember I said I was about to refuel it? That chopper was just about bone-dry. If the police hadn't shot it down, it wouldn't have gone much more than a mile anyway—max. I can't figure out how so little fuel could make such a big bang."

"Did you tell that to the police?" Nancy said, astonished at the sudden twist in the story of Johnson's getaway.

"Sure did," Mac said, folding his arms across his chest. "What they do with the information is up to them. I guess as far as they were concerned, that fellow Johnson was dead and done with, and the money he stole was gone, too. You know, they found some of his clothes in the wreckage, and they were all bloodied up."

Nancy nodded her head slowly, thinking about Mac's story and Johnson's final moments. "Thanks for talking to us," she said.

"Anytime," Mac replied with a grin. "You need anything else, just give me a call, hear?"

A few moments later they were walking back to the car, each lost in his or her thoughts.

"What do you make of all that, Nancy?" Bess finally asked, breaking the silence.

"I've got to think about it," Nancy said.

George winked at Bess and Mark. "A great mind is at work," she whispered loudly.

"All I know is that helicopters don't just explode by themselves," Nancy said.

"Let's go back to my place," Mark suggested. "We can talk it out there."

They piled into Nancy's car and drove back

to town. When they arrived at Mark's apartment, Marie and Frances Bradford were out on their porch as usual. Everyone said hello before entering the door leading up to Mark's apartment.

As they filed upstairs, Bess shook her head. "This case is too hard for me. My brain feels fried. Do you have any soda in the fridge, Mark?"

Mark, deep in thought, didn't seem to hear. "We'll nail Johnson yet," he said, taking out his apartment key. When he tried to insert it in the lock, the door swung open.

"That's funny," he said, walking inside. "I'm sure I locked that door."

Nancy stepped in right behind him. "I don't know if funny is the right word for this," she said.

The room was a total shambles. Papers and clothes were scattered everywhere, and the lamps and table had been overturned.

Mark's apartment had been ransacked!

Chapter

Nine

MARK, IT LOOKS LIKE you had some uninvited visitors," Nancy said slowly. Her eyes moved from the upended desk to the bookshelves that had been emptied onto the floor.

"You can say that again," Mark murmured.

"Did you have anything valuable?" Bess asked, stepping into the apartment in wide-eyed horror.

"Valuable? Not really." Mark glanced into the bedroom, which was in similar disarray. "A pair of gold cuff links and a CD player. I'm not very far along in the worldly goods department."

"Your CD player is still here," George said, pointing. It was sitting undisturbed on a shelf near the window. "It doesn't look like it was touched."

"The cuff links were in a little wooden box," Mark said.

"This one?" Nancy asked, holding up a small box that had been tossed on the floor near the bedroom door.

"That's it." Mark took the box from Nancy, opened it, and pulled out a pair of cuff links. "Would you believe—they're still here."

"What about the file on Johnson and Anderson Industries?" Nancy asked, surveying the pile of papers scattered around the overturned table.

"I don't see that," he said. He riffled through the debris. "I need those papers!"

Nancy took charge. The first thing to do was talk to the Bradford sisters. "Mark, continue checking to see what's missing, but try not to disturb things too much until the police get here," she ordered. "Bess, can you call the police? George, let's go talk to the Bradford sisters. Maybe they heard something."

When they got downstairs, the porch was empty. "They aren't out," George said, puzzled. She walked around the other side of the porch to make sure.

Nancy knocked on their door.

A few moments later Marie Bradford opened the door. "Hello, girls," she said pleasantly, removing her headphones. "Can I help you with something?"

"I'm sorry to bring bad news," Nancy began, "but someone broke into Mark's apartment."

The older woman turned pale. "Are you sure? Frances!" she called in a trembling voice. "Come quickly! Nancy says someone broke into our tenant's apartment!"

Frances strode into the hallway behind her sister. "But that's impossible. We've been right here all day!"

"And you never heard anyone?" Nancy asked.

"No one!" Marie insisted.

Frances Bradford furrowed her brow and looked at her sister. "Wait, Marie—now that I think about it, I was out in the backyard for a while." She turned to Nancy and George. "But Marie was here on the porch the whole time. Isn't that right, Marie?"

"The whole time," Marie confirmed.

"Were you listening to your portable stereo today?" Nancy asked Marie Bradford.

Marie's bright eyes widened and her hand moved to her mouth in dismay. "Why, yes, I was," she murmured guiltily. "So I wouldn't have heard anything happen, would I?" She looked at her sister as if she had just done something horrible.

Frances patted Marie on the back. "That's all right, dear. It's not your fault."

George touched Nancy lightly on the arm. "Someone's coming."

Nancy turned to see a young woman cutting across the lawn to the front walk.

"It's our niece, Linda," Frances explained to George and Nancy. "She said she'd come by today if she got off work early."

Linda was a pretty blond girl of about twenty-two. She wore a crisp black-and-white suit and black high heels. Nancy recalled the conversation she had had with Linda when she called Crabtree. Now she would finally meet Mark's ex-girlfriend face-to-face.

"Hi, Aunt Marie! Hello, Aunt Frances!" Linda said, waving as she made her way up the steps to the porch.

"Oh, Linda, thank goodness you're here!" Marie said, stepping from the doorway and pushing past Nancy and George. "You won't believe what just happened!"

Marie proceeded to fill her niece in on the whole story, with Frances wringing her hands beside her.

"Poor Mark," Linda said with a sigh. "He just can't seem to stay out of trouble. I wonder what it's about this time." She glanced curiously at Nancy and George.

"Linda, dear, have you met our neighbor George? And this is her friend, Nancy Drew." Frances made the introductions.

Linda smiled pleasantly at the two girls. "Pleased to meet you," she said, extending her hand politely.

Nancy said hello in a slightly deeper voice than normal. She didn't want Linda to connect her with the person who'd called Crabtree for a reference about Mark.

Just then, a police cruiser pulled up to the curb, and the two officers inside climbed out. "Oh, dear, we'd better show them upstairs," Marie said.

"I'll go inside and make you some tea," Linda offered quickly. "And, Aunt Marie, please don't mention to Mark that I'm here." Turning to Nancy and George, Linda said in a low voice, "Mark and I used to go together. I'm fond of him, of course, but I don't want to give him the impression that I'm interested in seeing him again."

Nancy nodded politely, as if it were all news to her. "Uh, George, maybe we'd better help out upstairs," she suggested. The police officers had gone up, following the Bradford sisters.

Upstairs, Mark was pacing in his rooms. The Bradford sisters were clucking over the state of the apartment.

"Nothing is missing," Mark announced.

"Nothing! I even found the Anderson files. They were right under the desk."

Nancy cautioned Mark to be quiet. It wouldn't do anyone any good to tell the police about the case they were working on. Mark instantly stopped talking.

The police began to search through the ransacked rooms. One told the two Bradford sisters that they could wait downstairs. He wrote Nancy's, George's, and Bess's names in his notebook and told them they could go.

"Mark, if you need anything, call me at home, okay?" said Nancy.

"Okay, Nancy," Mark said miserably. He came close to her and whispered, "I'd just like to know what they wanted!"

Nancy patted him on the back. "We'll talk later," she said.

They headed downstairs with the Bradford sisters. Stepping onto the porch, Nancy moved to avoid a small pile of potting soil that had been spilled from the planter.

"Now, look at that," Marie Bradford said, reaching for the broom that leaned against the wall of the house. "I spent all morning cleaning this porch. I don't know how I missed that spot." Vigorously, she swept up the dirt.

Frances Bradford walked the girls to the sidewalk and said goodbye.

"Where are we going now, Nan?" George asked.

"Downtown," Nancy answered, climbing into the car. "I've been thinking about the embezzled money. I want to check out a few things."

"Such as?" Bess asked after she'd gotten into the back seat. George got into the front seat beside Nancy.

"Remember, Mark told us that Johnson had a million dollars in cash when he was trying to make his getaway," Nancy said.

"That sure is a lot of money to be carrying around," George commented. "I'd be afraid of losing it."

"Or having it stolen," Bess added.

"Exactly," Nancy agreed, "Well, let's say that somehow Johnson wasn't killed in that crash. And that the money is still around."

Beth leaned into the front seat, clearly intrigued. "What do you mean?"

"I mean that the money could still be somewhere in River Heights."

Bess threw herself back into her seat and heaved a disappointed sigh. "Somewhere!" she said. "But how could we ever find it?"

"I don't know," Nancy had to admit. "But there's got to be a way." She drove downtown and pulled the car into a metered spot across from the post office, and the three girls got out.

"You two might as well do some window-shopping," Nancy suggested. "I can meet you at the pizza place later. I'll fill you in then."

Bess pouted. "She's trying to get rid of us, George."

"What exactly are you going to be doing, Nancy?" George prodded.

"Talking to a banker about opening an account," Nancy said casually.

"Bo-ring!" Bess sang out. All three girls burst out laughing.

When George and Bess had gone, Nancy stood on the post office steps and tried to imagine herself in the shoes of a man on the run. A man carrying a million dollars in cash in a suitcase. Where would I put it for safe-keeping, she asked herself.

There was only one bank in her line of vision—River Heights Savings Bank, an old and elegant institution with granite columns on either side of the main entrance. Nancy thought of something her father had told her when she was a little girl—the best hiding place is in plain sight because that's where people never think to look.

Nancy glanced at her watch. It was almost three. The bank would soon be closed for the day. Smoothing her hair, she strode across the street and ducked inside.

The atmosphere inside the bank was cool and hushed. A bald man with a bow tie sat at a service desk. As Nancy approached him, her heels clicked on the polished terrazzo floor.

"Do you wish to open an account?" he asked her, gesturing to the chair beside his desk.

"I'm not sure," said Nancy, sitting down. "Actually I have some valuables that I'd like to keep safe."

The man beamed. "Well, you've come to the right place. Now, which is more important to you, being discreet or earning interest?"

"Discretion, definitely," Nancy replied.

"I see." The man pursed his lips. "Well, then, I recommend a safety deposit box."

Nancy cocked her head. "Why is that?" she asked.

"First, because they're completely private," said the man, adjusting his bow tie. "You will be the only person to have access to the box. You will receive a key—the only key. Like this one." He held up a silver key with the bank's logo on it.

"And when can I use the box?" Nancy asked.

"During regular banking hours, of course," the clerk told her, adding, "That includes our new Saturday morning hours."

"Saturday morning? Isn't that unusual for a bank?" Nancy couldn't help asking.

"It's getting quite common," he announced. "It's for our customers' convenience. We're just keeping up with the times. So, shall I start filling out the forms?"

Nancy got up. "Thank you. You've been

very helpful. I've got another appointment right now, though. I'll come back later to open the box." Giving the clerk an apologetic smile, she hurried from the bank.

Nancy emerged into the bright afternoon sunshine with a sense of accomplishment. A safety deposit box would have been the perfect place for Johnson to hide the money. He'd have the only key. Was a key what that man had been searching for in the old Chinese desk?

While she pondered the different pieces of the puzzle, a sharp light flashed in her eyes. She raised her head. The light came from a top floor window of a building across the square. The sun was reflecting off something in the window.

At that moment the reflection disappeared, and Nancy could make out a man holding a pair of binoculars in the open window. He lowered them and stood still, staring down at her.

His was a face Nancy recognized—the man Mark Rubin had identified as J. Christopher Johnson!

Chapter

Ten

$\mathbf{H}$ER HEART POUNDING, Nancy stared up at the man in the window. Johnson, or whoever he was, watched her for a moment longer, then abruptly moved away from the window.

"Hi, Nancy!"

Spinning around, Nancy saw Bess and George coming toward her on the sidewalk.

"What's wrong?" George asked, seeing the startled expression on her friend's face.

"I just saw Johnson," Nancy cried, her heart racing. "Up there!" She pointed to the empty window.

"I don't see anybody," Bess said.

"We haven't got a minute to lose," Nancy said, hustling her friends across the street.

When they reached the front door of the building, she said, "You two go around to the back and cover it. I'll go in the front."

Bess and George raced through the parking lot on one side of the building. Nancy strode in the front entrance. Pulling open the metal door, she walked into a small, dirty foyer with yellowing walls.

A black directory hung over a set of smudged buttons and a gritty intercom. There were few names on it, and most of them had missing letters. Each floor had two apartments, one marked *F* and the other *R*. That had to mean front and rear, Nancy thought. She reached for the red button marked 6F, since the man had been watching her from the top-floor front apartment.

There was no answer. Pressing the buzzer for 6F again, Nancy waited. Still no answer. She pulled hard on the inside door that led to the first floor corridor and a stairwell. Despite its battered condition, it was securely locked.

Nancy considered, then pressed the button marked 6R. Almost immediately the lock on the inside door buzzed ferociously. She pushed it open. Taking the steps two at a time, she raced up to the top floor. A pasty-faced woman in a flower-printed dress stood in an open doorway at one end of the hallway.

"Are you the social worker?" she demanded.

"No," Nancy answered. "I came to see your neighbor, actually. Do you know if he's home?"

The woman was visibly annoyed. "Fat chance," she said, turning back to her apartment.

"Wait a minute," Nancy said, gulping to catch her breath after running up six flights. "I'm sure I saw him at the window as I was walking over here."

"Look, I don't know nothing about nothing," the woman said. "I stay out of their way, and they stay out of mine, know what I mean?"

"Sure, I know what you mean." Nancy nodded. "But, see, Mr. Johnson wanted to hire me to paint his apartment. I misplaced the apartment number." She pointed to 6F. "Is that Mr. Johnson's?"

"Johnson? Never heard of him," the woman snapped. "You got the wrong building."

"Maybe I got the name wrong," Nancy said, trying to be as pleasant as possible.

"Maybe you mean Wilson," the woman told her.

Nancy slapped her forehead. "Of course! Mr. Wilson."

"Well, it beats me why he wants his apartment painted. It isn't like he's around to enjoy it, if you know what I mean."

"Why?" Nancy said, puzzled. "Did he go somewhere?"

The woman stared. "Honey, he sure did. He's in jail downtown!" She glanced furtively down the hallway to see if anyone else was within hearing distance and lowered her voice. "And, honey, if you want my advice, I'd steer clear of any painting jobs for him. If you want to get paid, that is."

Nancy looked indignant. "He's broke?"

"He's as crooked as they come," the woman said forcefully.

"I can't believe it! He was so pleasant when I met him. He's a medium tall man of about thirty-five, right?" Nancy probed. "With a mustache?"

The woman shot her a puzzled look. "He was thirty-five a long time ago," she said crossly. "Artie Wilson is sixty if he's a day. Honey, you got the wrong guy." Without another word, she stepped back and shut the door.

Nancy waited a moment, thinking what to do next. She walked to the far end of the hallway and knocked on the door of 6F. No response. Putting her hand gingerly on the doorknob, she turned it. It was locked.

It's probably just as well, Nancy thought. If Johnson really was in there, he wouldn't give me a friendly reception.

Reluctantly, Nancy turned around and began to go down the stairs. Who is Artie Wilson? she wondered. And what was Johnson doing in his apartment—if it was Johnson that she had seen at the window. She rounded the second-floor stairwell and headed for the final flight of stairs.

"Stop right there," growled an angry male voice.

Fear shot through Nancy. When she turned around, though, she realized immediately that this wasn't the man she'd seen in the window. This one had curly black hair, dark skin, and piercing dark eyes.

"You selling something?" he demanded, blocking her way.

Nancy stepped back. "Selling?"

"We don't allow door-to-door salespeople in this building. I'm the super here, and I want you out on the double."

"Actually, I was looking for someone who lives here," Nancy said.

"Who?" the building superintendent demanded.

"The tenant in Six-F," Nancy told him. "Artie Wilson."

"What are you from, the probation department or something?"

"I'm from social services," said Nancy, silently thanking the woman in 6R for the inspiration. "I've been assigned to Mr. Wilson's case. I'm trying to help him get a job."

The man looked Nancy up and down. "You seem a little young to be a social worker."

"Maybe," Nancy said coldly. "Do you have any idea when Mr. Wilson will be in?"

"You know he's in jail?" the super said sharply, still eyeing Nancy with suspicion.

"Well, yes, of course. Or rather, he was. Isn't he out now?"

"You got your dates mixed up. He's still in the slammer downtown. But I heard he was going to be out real soon." The super snickered. "Good luck finding him a job. He isn't exactly the hardworking type."

The super started down the last flight of stairs and Nancy followed. "He was in prison for robbery, wasn't he?" she asked, taking a wild guess and hoping that it wasn't too far off.

The super laughed. "You government people sure get things mixed up. No, he doesn't have the guts for something like that. Wilson's a specialist." They reached the first floor landing. "He was in for forgery. Had a regular factory up there cranking out phony IDs, social security cards, driver's licenses, passports, the whole bit."

Nancy snapped her fingers. "Of course, it was stupid of me to forget. And I just read his file this morning."

"Yeah, well, read it again," the super told her. He opened the door and motioned for her to leave by jerking his head toward the street.

Nancy stepped out into the late afternoon sun. Forgery? She shook her head, mystified. Once again she looked up at the sixth-floor windows. They were empty. But the open window where she had spotted the man watching her was now closed.

Whatever the super and the woman in 6R said, someone had been in that apartment. And if what they'd told her was true, it wasn't Artie Wilson.

Bess and George trotted around the side of the building and ran up to her.

"What happened?" George asked anxiously.

"You first," Nancy said. "Did anyone leave the building through the back door?"

George shook her head. "Nope. Not that we saw, and we've been standing there ever since you went inside."

"How about you, Nan? Find anybody?" Bess asked.

"I found out there's a forger by the name of Artie Wilson who lives in the apartment where I saw the man in the window. But he's in prison."

"So do you believe Mark now?" George asked. "Do you actually think Johnson is alive?"

Nancy pursed her lips and nodded. "It certainly seems like a possibility."

Bess let out a low whistle. "But how, Nancy? After a helicopter explosion like that?"

"That's the next thing we're going to find out, Bess," Nancy told her friend. They had reached her car and she stopped at the curb. "Wait right here, you two. I want to make a few phone calls. I won't be long."

Nancy trotted over to a nearby telephone booth. Her first call was to Mark at the pizza parlor.

"Hi, Nancy. I'm on the other line. Can I call you back?" he asked.

"This'll just take a minute," she told him. "I wanted you to know I'm going to charter a helicopter for tomorrow night. I want to duplicate Johnson's last ride. It may teach us something."

"Good idea," Mark said. "It worked when we found those mangled sunglasses."

"I'll call you to let you know the time," she said before she hung up.

Nancy's second call was to Mac MacIlvaney. "Mac? I need to charter a helicopter for tomorrow night. I'd like to go up at exactly the same time Johnson made his ride."

"That would be about seven-fifteen," he answered. "What's this all about?"

"I'll fill you in tomorrow night, Mac," she

said, quickly hanging up. She made a third phone call to Chief McGinnis at the River Heights Police Department and managed to catch him just as he was leaving for the day.

"Arthur Wilson?" McGinnis said when Nancy inquired about the forger. "A convicted felon, as I recall. Hang on, I'll see what I can find out."

A minute later the chief came back on the line. "Yup, we got him here, Nancy. He violated his parole in a minor way, so a judge ordered him to serve another two months of his sentence. He's due out in two days, on Friday at five o'clock."

"Any chance I can visit him in jail before then?" Nancy asked.

"During regular visiting hours, sure." McGinnis sounded alarmed. "Say, what do you want to see him for? He's not a pleasant character."

"Just following my nose," Nancy told him. "I have one more question—did you ever lab test Johnson's bloody clothing after the explosion?"

"No, I don't think so. Why?"

"Chief, I'm beginning to believe Christopher Johnson is still alive," Nancy said. "I've got to go, but I'll keep you posted on what I find out."

Nancy hung up and ran back to where Bess and George were standing. "Big day tomorrow," Nancy told them. "Want to come out to the airport with me at around dusk?"

"Sure, Nancy," Bess said. "Why?"

"We're going on a helicopter ride," Nancy said with a mischievous grin.

Late the next morning Nancy drove to the River Heights Jail and asked to see Artie Wilson.

"You have twenty minutes," the guard said, ushering her into the waiting area. "The prisoner will come into cubicle fourteen. You can speak to him through the Plexiglas screen."

Nancy seated herself on a hard plastic chair and waited. In a few minutes a thin, stooped, white-haired man appeared on the other side of the window. He cast Nancy a dark look and sat down.

"Artie Wilson?" Nancy asked, meeting his cold gaze with her own cool stare.

"Yeah," the man answered, sticking his chin out defiantly. "Who wants to know?"

"I'm here to find out what happened to the money that was embezzled from the Anderson corporation," Nancy said quietly.

Her bold statement obviously startled Wilson, but his expression immediately hardened into a sullen stare.

"What's it to you?" he demanded, his lip curling.

"The question is, what's it to you?" Nancy shot back, keeping her gaze level and steady.

Wilson slouched in his chair. "Let me tell you something, young lady. I don't know who you are, but I don't like people sticking their noses in where they don't belong."

"You're in touch with Christopher Johnson," Nancy bluffed. "I know he's alive. And I also know he's hiding out at your apartment."

Wilson blanched. His hands began to tremble, and he dropped them to his lap. "I don't have to talk to you," he spat. "I don't even know who you are, lady."

He leaned close to the Plexiglas, his eyes flashing. "I'm not saying Johnson's alive, and I'm not saying he's dead. But I'll tell you this. If you know what's good for you, keep your nose out of other people's business—or you could end up getting hurt real bad!"

Chapter

Eleven

NANCY DIDN'T FLINCH. So Artie Wilson was threatening her—or warning her, she thought. Well, she'd heard threats before. She stood and pushed her chair back.

"Nice talking to you, Mr. Wilson," she said coolly.

"I've lived a long time by keeping my mouth shut," Wilson snarled. "I advise you to do the same."

The guard approached and put his hand on Wilson's arm. Wilson walked away.

Nancy watched him go. She still didn't know how to connect a convicted forger to Christopher Johnson's crime, and the whole case was beginning to frustrate her. Maybe that night, though, she'd learn something at the airport, if all went well.

Fifteen minutes later Nancy was pulling into her driveway. Hannah Gruen was standing at the front door, taking in the mail.

"Well, hello, stranger," Hannah greeted her.

Nancy gave her a quick hug and a kiss. "I know I've been out a lot lately. Sorry."

Hannah opened the door and gestured for Nancy to enter ahead of her. "I'm sure you're keeping yourself busy. I hope you're hungry. I just made some chicken salad and fresh iced tea."

Nancy got a plate while Hannah put out the food. "Your father has been concerned," Hannah told her. "Where did you go in the middle of the night Monday?"

"I was totally safe," Nancy assured her, digging into the delicious chicken salad. "I was at the police station in Brewster." She knew that Hannah had probably been even more worried than her father, but Hannah would never admit it.

"Well, I'm happy to hear that," Hannah said. "More salad?"

"No thanks. Any calls?"

"Yes—Ned called," Hannah told her. "He said he would be in his room this afternoon, if you want to reach him." She handed Nancy a napkin. "I guess he's expecting you this week-end."

Oh, no, Nancy thought. She'd forgotten all about going to visit Ned at Emerson College that weekend. And with the pace of the investigation quickening, she knew she'd have to cancel. She felt terrible, even though she knew Ned would understand.

Taking the stairs two at a time, Nancy went to her room and reached for her phone. Ned answered on the second ring.

"I knew it was you," he said. "I miss you. I can hardly wait to see you on the weekend."

"Ned, look," Nancy said with a sigh. "I'm sorry but—"

Ned listened as she filled him in on the case. When she was through, he let out a sigh.

"I understand, Nancy. These sound like dangerous characters, though. Are you sure you're not taking any unnecessary chances?"

Nancy let out a frustrated sigh. "What's going on? All of a sudden, everybody's worried about me—and I'm not in any danger at all!"

There was a beat of silence at the other end of the line. Then Ned asked, "Who else is worried about you? This guy Mark?"

Nancy wasn't sure, but she thought she detected a note of jealousy in his voice. "Not Mark," she answered with a giggle. "He's too involved in this case to worry about anybody, including himself."

"What's he like, anyway?" Ned asked.

"He's very cute," Nancy teased. "But I

99

already have a boyfriend, remember?" She laughed. "Even though I can't get to see him this weekend."

The reassurance seemed to work. "Well, the weekend afterward for sure," he urged. "And I'll call you before then. I love you."

"I love you, too," she whispered, and hung up the phone with a wistful sigh.

Nancy passed the afternoon cleaning her room and writing a letter to her aunt Eloise. Finally it was time to pick up George, Bess, and Mark for the trip to the airport.

The cousins were both on the Bradfords' porch chatting with Frances and Marie. Nancy beeped the horn. As George got into the front seat next to Nancy, Bess stood beside the window.

"Nan, I can't come with you," she said, guiltily. "This guy Scott that I have a total crush on asked me out for tonight. What could I say? That I couldn't come because I had to go up in a helicopter and fly over a cornfield?"

"Hey, don't worry about it, Bess," Nancy said with a grin. "Just have fun, and tell us all about it tomorrow."

Bess was obviously relieved. "You know I will. Have a good time, okay?" With a last wave, she took off for her house.

Nancy grinned at George and shook her head. "Good old Bess, huh?"

"I think Bess is secretly scared to go up in a helicopter," George commented.

Seconds later Mark burst out his front door and almost tripped down the porch steps. George leaned forward in her seat so he could crawl into the back of the Mustang.

"Listen," he said when he was settled. "I have something to say before we head off."

"What?" Nancy said, turning to face him.

Mark leaned forward in his seat. "I've been thinking maybe I should do this helicopter ride myself, Nancy. It could be dangerous, and I don't want you getting hurt because of me. I mean, it's my case, after all."

Nancy rolled her eyes. "That's very gallant of you," she said with more than a hint of sarcasm. "But George and I can handle ourselves just fine."

"We've probably been in a lot more tight fixes than you have, Mark," George pointed out. "Besides, going up in the helicopter was Nancy's idea, not yours."

Mark glanced from George to Nancy. "You're right." He nodded. "But I was thinking, if we really want to reconstruct Johnson's escape, we should probably do a real chase. We could ask the police to fire a couple of shots to—"

"Planet Earth to Mark Rubin!" Nancy broke in. "Do you read us?" Mark blinked.

Nancy grinned at him. "Just trying to bring you down to earth again."

Mark nodded and sat back. "Sorry," he said. "I guess I got a little carried away.

"Okay, so forget I even said it and listen to my big breakthrough," Mark went on. He looked from Nancy to George with a self-satisfied grin, deliberately keeping them in suspense.

"No fair, Mark," Nancy cried. "Out with it!"

Mark reached into his pocket and took out the pair of mangled glasses Nancy had found at the railroad tracks. He dangled them in front of the two girls. "One lens was completely smashed, but there was enough glass left in the left lens for an optometrist to tell me its strength."

"So?" George prodded.

"So then I took the day off from work and spent all afternoon calling every eye doctor in Brewster until I found Johnson's. I sweet-talked the receptionist into telling me his prescription."

Nancy's eyes lit up. "Was it—"

Mark nodded slowly and deliberately. "It matched. Exactly. These are Johnson's glasses. They have to be."

"So that proves it!" George exclaimed. "You *did* see him and he *is* still alive!"

Mark pretended to be insulted. "Did you ever doubt me?"

Nancy and George couldn't help laughing. "Let's just say we had to look at all the angles first," Nancy said.

"That still doesn't explain how he survived a helicopter explosion," George pointed out.

Nancy started the car. "That, my friends, is what we'll find out before the day is over."

"Well, drive on, Jeeves—to the airport!" Mark waved his arms to signal Nancy to go forward.

When they arrived at the airport, a helicopter sat on the landing pad. Nancy and her friends got out of the car and hurried over. Mac waved and called, "You're right on time!"

He threw an adjustable wrench back into a toolbox, closed the lid, and hoisted it into the fuselage. He motioned Nancy, George, and Mark to climb aboard, while he circled the aircraft and got into the pilot's seat. Nancy, George, and Mark climbed into the passenger seats.

"Mac, I'd like you to take the exact route Johnson took the night he stole your helicopter," Nancy said. "When we get to the cornfield, can you just hover so we can get a good look?"

"No sweat," Mac said, his hands moving quickly among the chopper's controls. The engine caught, and the rotor began to turn, slowly at first. It speeded up until it was a blur. The airstream pounded into the ground and filled the cabin, fluttering the passengers' hair and clothing. Mac adjusted the controls. The next thing Nancy knew, the pad fell away beneath them.

She gazed out the open side door. Below them, she saw fields of fresh green corn, mixed with others of yellow hay.

"The chopper crashed near Hoffner's farmhouse, about a half mile that way," Mac shouted over the sound of the motor, pointing left to a group of farm buildings in the distance.

Nancy saw a patch of black in a cornfield not far away. "I think I see the place it went down, out to the left."

"That's it," Mac answered, veering in the direction Nancy was looking. As he steered, the chopper descended, passing barely twenty feet above some haystacks next to a dirt road.

"How high was Johnson flying?" Nancy asked.

"About as high as we are now," Mac told her. The airstream from the helicopter's rotor blew the rows of corn almost flat to the ground.

"I see it now, too," George said, pointing to where the corn had been burned away in a large circle.

"Where?" Mark asked anxiously. He stood

shakily and moved toward the doorway to peer out.

"Over there," George pointed.

Mark braced himself in the doorway and stuck his head out of the chopper. "Where?"

"Don't lean out like that," Nancy warned.

"I'm okay," Mark shouted, his head still half out the open door. His hand closed tightly around a grip on the wall of the fuselage.

"I'll swing us around so you'll get a better look," Mac told them, steadying his gaze as he began to turn the helicopter. "Move back in for a minute, son."

"I still don't see it!" Mark was yelling. He leaned out even farther. Suddenly the helicopter bucked in a gust of heavy wind.

"I said, get back in here!" Mac yelled.

Nancy gasped as Mark's left hand suddenly slipped from its hold on the wall.

"Mark!" she cried. Moving together, she and George grabbed at Mark's trousers and pulled him back into the craft just before he slipped out.

"Yikes!" Mark yelled. He fell back into the copter and crashed against the back of Mac's seat. The helicopter veered on an angle to the left and Mac's tool kit slid out from under the seat.

"Thanks, Nancy," Mark said, scrambling to retrieve the tool kit and put it back. "Hey, what's this?" A small black case had drifted out from under the seat where the toolbox had been.

Mac glanced over his shoulder at the case. "I never saw that before," he called.

Mark scrutinized the case. He flicked the metal latch open with his thumb. Then his eyes widened and his face went white.

Nancy craned her neck and looked inside the case. A small, digital timer was connected by wire and tape to a bundle of round sticks.

"It's a bomb!" Mark shouted with horror.

Nancy's mouth went dry. It was a bomb! The square red numbers were quickly counting down to zero—and there were only twenty-four seconds left before it exploded!

Chapter
Twelve

Nancy made a split-second decision. "Give it to me, Mark," she ordered. Taking the case in both hands and holding it as far from her body as she could, she inched to the door.

"Mac, be ready to get us out of here," she called to the pilot.

"You say the word, kid," Mac replied through tightly clenched teeth.

"Hold on to me," Nancy told Mark when she was standing in the open doorway. "Tight. Grab on to my waist and don't let me go. Hurry!"

Mark slid a strong arm around Nancy's slender body and held her fast. With his other hand, he clutched the metal handle on the wall of the fuselage.

"Now, Mac!" Nancy shouted, letting the bomb fly out into space.

Instantly, the veteran pilot let out the throttle and pulled the chopper in the opposite direction.

Ka-boom! The bomb hit the cornfield twenty feet below and exploded like thunder, sending a powerful shock wave through the helicopter. Nancy, George, and Mark were hurled to the floor.

The chopper began veering crazily. Looking up at the cockpit, Nancy saw to her horror that MacIlvaney was slumped sideways in his seat. He was out cold! Nobody was at the controls!

The helicopter swerved back and forth, vibrating horribly. Nancy clawed her way slowly to the front and sat in the copilot's seat. There were identical controls to the ones Mac had been using. Although Nancy had a pilot's license for small aircraft, she knew that flying a helicopter was quite different from flying an airplane.

She grabbed a control lever that she had seen Mac using earlier and imitated the movements she remembered him making. But instead of lifting the chopper higher, it plunged toward the ground.

Keeping her cool, Nancy jammed the lever away from her. The helicopter righted itself.

"Wake up, Mac!" Nancy screamed. "I need you."

Mac must have heard her because he opened his eyes just then. For a brief second he looked stunned. Then the realization of what was happening flooded into his face. He leaped forward in his seat and grabbed the controls. Almost instantly the helicopter rose and leveled off. Her hands shaking, Nancy released her grip on the lever she'd been working.

"Where's Mark?" George shouted from the cabin behind them. "He's gone! He must have fallen out."

Nancy stood up in the copilot's seat to search behind her. Just as George had said, Mark was nowhere to be seen. A feeling of dread rose in the pit of her stomach.

"Hold on," Mac shouted, yanking one of the controls toward him.

The helicopter turned almost sideways and veered around in a tight circle. Mac slowed it down and flew low over the cornfield. A small fire was burning where the bomb had exploded, and smoke swirled into the sky. Just as they passed over a haystack, George shouted.

"I think I see him!"

Nancy peered through the windscreen. She saw something moving on top of the haystack. A moment later, Mark's head popped up through the straw. "There he is!" she yelled.

Mac saw the young man and slowed the chopper more. He descended gradually and brought the aircraft to hover a few feet over the haystack. Nancy crawled back to the cabin and helped George pull Mark aboard.

His face was white and he was barely able to speak.

"Mark, you are one lucky guy," George scolded when he was back inside.

He nodded in agreement. "If it hadn't been for that haystack, I'd have broken every bone in my body."

"You can say that again," Nancy commented. "But congratulations, anyway."

"Congratulations?" Mark and George exclaimed together, staring at Nancy as if she were crazy.

Nancy nodded. "You just gave us a demonstration of how Johnson got away."

When George and Mark both began to speak at once, Nancy raised a hand. "Wait until we get back to the airport," she told them.

Mac soon had the helicopter on the landing pad at the airport.

"Whew," George said when they had landed. "That was not fun."

As she stepped out onto the runway, Nancy felt a huge wave of relief roll over her. "Good old solid ground. I don't know when I've appreciated you so much." She hugged George tightly. "We almost bought the farm, George."

"I guess our number just wasn't up yet, huh?" George said with a forced grin.

"Is anybody else's stomach a little jumpy?" Mark asked. He was still gray.

"Come on," Nancy suggested, taking Mark gently by the elbow and pulling him forward. "Let's find a place to sit down."

"You can use the lounge next to my office, Nancy," Mac told them. "I'm going to call the police."

As they approached the hangar, they watched two police cars and two fire engines sail into the parking lot, their lights blinking madly and their sirens wailing. Someone had obviously alerted them already.

Mark took a deep breath when they entered the hangar. "I'm starting to feel better," he said softly.

Half a dozen police officers and four fire fighters entered the hangar from the side door. The fire fighters spoke with George and Mark, and Nancy talked with the police. She was surprised to see that Chief McGinnis was one of them.

"Chief! What are you doing here?" she asked.

"Your housekeeper told me I'd find you here," he told her. He turned to Mac. "I saw the explosion across the fields as we were driving out here and radioed for backup. Is everyone all right?"

Mac nodded and turned to Nancy. "This

young lady did a fine job out there, Chief. She saved our lives, in fact. Now, would someone mind telling me what's going on?"

The police chief turned his attention on Nancy. "I thought it was about time you and I had a little talk about the Anderson Industries case."

"My friends and I may be able to help you with it," she told the chief. "We've been working on it for several days, and we're starting to make some breakthroughs."

The chief let out a sigh. "Do these so-called breakthroughs have anything to do with the explosion that just about killed all of you a few minutes ago?"

Nancy nodded. "How did you know?"

The chief sighed. "First you called me up and asked about the helicopter explosion. The next day you want to know all about a convicted forger named Arthur Wilson. And you tell me you think Christopher Johnson could still be alive. Now, I've known you long enough to know when you're involved in a case." McGinnis looked at Nancy. "Why don't you fill me in?"

Nancy swallowed. She introduced Mark, who had finished with the fire chief, to McGinnis and told him about Mark's experience at Crabtree. "I got involved because Mark was sure he'd spotted Johnson—even though he was supposed to be dead."

112

Quickly Nancy filled Chief McGinnis in on the details of her case. He listened attentively, occasionally nodding.

When she was finished he said, "I'll have a man get a search warrant for Artie Wilson's apartment to look for Johnson. Now, what exactly were you up to out here?"

"We made this helicopter run to see how Johnson might have survived," Nancy told him. "Of course, we didn't expect it to be so realistic."

McGinnis narrowed his eyes. "And did you figure it out?"

Nancy looked at Mark and George, then back at the chief. She nodded. "Can I ask you one question first, Chief?"

McGinnis nodded.

"It's about the bloodied clothing you found in the wreckage after the helicopter blew up."

"Sheep's blood," the chief said. "I had the crime lab test it this morning, after talking to you."

Nancy nodded. "It was a well-planned get-away," she said. "First Johnson built a bomb with a timer. While he was in the air, he changed his clothing and left his old clothes on board, soaked in animal blood. He came over the fields low and bailed out onto a haystack. The helicopter kept going until the bomb blew it up. That way Johnson didn't have to have a body. After the fuss died down, Johnson made his way to River Heights."

Chief McGinnis nodded with satisfaction. "It's all beginning to make sense," he said. "Let me fill in a few missing details for you. Johnson was in the naval air corps when he was a young man. He knew how to fly a chopper, and he had experience with all kinds of explosive devices."

"Whew!" George said. "He sounds more like a guerrilla fighter than a real estate executive."

"That's not such a wild comparison," McGinnis replied. His brow wrinkled with concern. "In fact, it's very appropriate. Let me give you all a word of warning. Christopher Johnson is a ruthless customer. He'll stop at nothing to get what he wants."

"We'll be okay," Mark assured him.

"There are just a few more things we need to check out," Nancy added.

"I know better than to try to talk you out of investigating a case, Nancy," the chief said, "but next time, come to me before it gets dangerous. Is that clear?"

"I promise," Nancy said.

When Chief McGinnis said they could go, Nancy drove Mark and George back to River Heights. They stopped at Bess's house to see if their friend was back from her date. She was, and she waved them into the Marvins' comfortable living room, where they flopped down on the overstuffed sofa and easy chairs.

Nancy listened with half an ear as Bess gave them all the details of her date. She was thinking hard, and some of the pieces of the puzzle were starting to fall into place.

"So how was the helicopter ride?" Bess inquired at last.

George and Mark quickly filled her in. Her big blue eyes grew increasingly wider.

"You were almost killed!" she exclaimed when they were done.

"But we weren't, thanks to Nancy." Mark turned to her. "You're amazing," he exclaimed, getting up and planting a kiss on the top of her head. "Not only did you save us, but you turned my klutziness into something that helped you figure out a piece of the puzzle."

"Mark, it's time to stop thinking of yourself as a klutz. The fact is, you've done a fantastic job on this investigation from day one," Nancy told him. "You haven't made a wrong move yet."

"Except that when I had Johnson, I blew it," Mark said, with a frown.

"I think I know what Nancy's getting at, Mark!" George put in. Her brown eyes opened wide as realization struck. "You *didn't* blow the case. Johnson must have had advance warning." She checked Nancy for confirmation of her idea.

"That's right." Nancy nodded. "Johnson had an accomplice. Someone helped him. Someone warned him. And someone alerted him to the fact that we were going up in that helicopter tonight. The big question now is— who?"

Chapter

Thirteen

THE FOUR SAT IN SILENCE for a minute, thinking over Nancy's question.

"Could Mac have let the information slip innocently, Nancy?" George suggested at last. "He might have left our names on a log in his office in a place where anybody could see them."

"That's possible, I suppose," Nancy said, although she was unconvinced. "But it wouldn't explain all the other things Johnson seems to have known about. Let's see, who else knew about our ride? Aside from Hannah and Ned, I didn't tell a soul."

"The only ones I told were my parents," George said.

"*I* didn't say anything," Bess piped up.

"Well—" Mark gulped. A flush started creeping up his face from his throat. "I, um, actually told a couple of people we were coming out here tonight."

Everyone turned to him.

"Well, I didn't say why I was going up in a helicopter," he said, defending himself. "It's just that someone at the pizza place asked me what I was doing tonight."

"You said you told a couple of people," Nancy probed. "Who else?"

"Well, I mentioned it at work, so there were several people around, including a few customers. But I didn't recognize any of them."

"That's just great," George muttered sarcastically.

"And then there were the Bradford sisters," Mark continued. "They were on the porch this morning, and we started chatting. Me and my big mouth. Oh, and I told Linda, too, last night when we were on the phone. But I'm sure she didn't tell anyone."

"Okay," Nancy said, "There's no sense in getting upset about what's already happened. Just be more careful in the future, okay, Mark?"

"Sure will," Mark promised, his head still hanging.

"Can we go now?" George asked. "I'm beat."

"Yes," Nancy said, standing up. "I want to

get a good night's sleep, if I can. Tomorrow's going to be busy."

"Oh?" Mark asked, intrigued.

"Chief McGinnis is going to have Artie Wilson's apartment searched," Nancy explained. "If Johnson is there, the case will be closed."

"That sounds a little vague," George said softly, walking with Nancy to the front door and holding it open. "It's not like you to just wait for the police to do something."

"I'll tell you later," Nancy whispered to George. Revealing her plans with Mark around didn't seem like the best idea at the moment.

The next morning Nancy was up early. Before breakfast she was on the phone to Chief McGinnis. He told her that his men had searched the Wilson apartment, and there were signs that someone had been living there. But it was empty when his men had arrived. Johnson had flown the coop again. Before he hung up, McGinnis once again warned Nancy to be careful.

"Thanks," she replied before saying goodbye. She hurried to the kitchen, toasted an English muffin, and ate it quickly.

"Will you be home for lunch, Nancy?" Hannah wanted to know.

"Not today, but I will see you tonight."

Blowing Hannah a kiss, Nancy grabbed her

car keys and tore out to the driveway. On the drive to Brewster, she went over the case. There were a few pieces of the puzzle missing, and the most important was the identity of Johnson's accomplice.

Since Johnson had been warned of the sting being set up by Crabtree, Nancy reasoned that it was logical to suspect someone within the agency. She needed to take a closer look at Crabtree and Company.

A little while later, she pulled into the underground parking lot under the office tower that housed Crabtree.

Her heels clicking on the polished granite floor, Nancy strode purposefully to the elevator and rode up to the agency offices on the nineteenth floor.

"I'd like to talk to Mr. Crabtree, as soon as possible," she told the receptionist, who sat behind an old-fashioned oak desk.

"Do you have an appointment?" the woman asked in a clipped tone.

"No, but I have some important information on the Anderson Industries case. It's rather urgent," Nancy added.

"Name, please," the receptionist murmured.

"Nancy Drew," Nancy replied.

Still looking at her with cool suspicion, the secretary used the intercom. "Mr. Crabtree, there's a young woman named Nancy Drew here to see you. She says it's in reference to the Anderson Industries case."

Soon Nancy was ushered into Archer Crabtree's large corner office. Crabtree was a tall, well-dressed man of about fifty, with silver hair and tired-looking brown eyes. "Well, what is it?" he asked.

After introducing herself, Nancy said, "I think you should know that Christopher Johnson is alive and has an accomplice inside this agency."

Crabtree shrugged nonchalantly. "Alive? Impossible! And if you're talking about Mark Rubin, he's already been fired."

"It's not Mark Rubin. It's someone else," Nancy said in a firm voice.

The executive became more interested. "Do you have any proof?"

"No—not exactly," Nancy said hesitantly. "But I do know that Johnson is still alive, and the police might be reopening the investigation." She deliberately fudged the information, not wanting to give away Chief McGinnis's intentions.

Crabtree held her eyes and his finger went to the intercom on his desk. "Get Hal Slade in here right away," he ordered. "Mr. Slade is the investigator who handled the Anderson Industries case."

"But, Mr. Crabtree," the receptionist protested. "Mr. Slade is with a client."

"I don't care if he's with the president of the United States, get him in here right now. Tell him it's urgent—it's about the Anderson case."

So, Nancy thought. It hadn't occurred to Mr. Crabtree that Slade might be the person they were after. Did that mean that Slade could be trusted—or did it just mean that Mr. Crabtree had overlooked him as a suspect?

Moments later an overweight man with thinning hair and watery eyes entered. He had Linda Bates in tow. "I brought Linda in so she could take notes," he told Crabtree, taking Nancy in curiously.

Linda, lovely as ever in a crisp blue business suit and pumps, had a pen and pad in her hand as she stepped forward. "Nancy!" she blurted out. "What are you doing here?"

"You know this woman?" Crabtree asked sharply.

"Yes," Linda answered softly. "She's a— friend of my aunts."

"I see." Crabtree settled down behind his desk and gazed at Nancy. "Now, tell us everything, but make it quick if you will. This is a busy agency, and we're busy people."

"Christopher Johnson has an accomplice, and it's someone who works in this agency," Nancy said, shifting her gaze from Crabtree to Slade.

"You mean 'had,' not 'has,'" Slade commented. "Mark Rubin's out, and Johnson's dead."

"No, he's not," Nancy told him. "He's alive."

"Oh?" Hal Slade challenged tersely. "And how do you know that?"

"He's been seen," Nancy said. "And the clothes the police found when Johnson's helicopter blew up didn't have Johnson's blood on them. It was sheep's blood. Johnson faked his death that night. He arranged for the helicopter to blow up after he'd already escaped."

Nancy noticed that Slade had become uncomfortable looking. She continued. "What's more, I'm convinced that Mark Rubin wasn't Johnson's accomplice. Last night Johnson or his accomplice tried to kill me and Mark because we were getting close to finding him."

"This sounds like a work of fiction to me, Mr. Crabtree," Slade snapped.

"Well, it sounds like it's worth looking into to me," Crabtree said, overruling him. "Our client, Anderson Industries, has lost a million dollars. That's reason enough to reopen the investigation."

"Then I'll get on it right away." Slade smiled at his boss.

Nancy caught his eye as he and Linda walked out of the office. Slade looked furious.

"Thank you for coming here, Miss Drew," Crabtree told her, standing up. "I've heard of some of your work in the past, which of course gives your information a certain weight. We'll look into this matter right away."

Nancy walked out into the reception area, where she found Linda Bates waiting for her. Slade was nowhere in sight.

"Nancy, I can't believe that about the explosion last night. It's awful. You could have been killed!" Linda said.

"Thankfully, I'm still around." Nancy smiled. Just as she turned toward the elevators, something occurred to her. She turned back to Linda. "By the way, Mark told you we were going up in the helicopter last night, didn't he?"

Linda seemed surprised, but then she nodded. "Yes, I guess he did," she agreed.

"Did you tell anyone?"

The blond woman shrugged. "No, I—" Suddenly her eyes widened. "Actually I did. I mentioned it to Hal, that's all."

Nancy forced a carefree smile. "Oh. Well, don't worry about it," she said. "I've got to go." She walked to the elevator and pressed the button for the garage. As soon as the doors closed and it began descending, Nancy felt excitement shoot through her.

She had certainly shaken things up at Crabtree. More than that, she thought she had a good idea who Johnson's accomplice was.

If Linda had told Hal Slade about their

helicopter trip, then Slade was the obvious connection to Johnson. Slade had been in a position to tip Johnson off about the sting as well. And Slade had certainly tried to keep Mark from investigating Johnson.

Yes, Nancy thought, it seemed as if the whole thing was a setup by Johnson and Slade from the very beginning.

She stepped off the elevator and pushed through the heavy door to the garage. Her car was several rows down, and she dug her keys out of her purse as she made her way toward it.

After getting into her car and fastening her seat belt, Nancy felt a hand grab her from behind. Someone was in the back seat! Strong fingers began to close around her neck.

"Don't bother screaming, Little Miss Detective," a male voice snarled. "No one can hear you down here."

Chapter

Fourteen

NANCY RECOGNIZED THE VOICE instantly. It was Hal Slade!

"What do you want?" she asked, unpleasantly aware of his fingers pressing into her skin.

Slade relaxed his grip slightly. "Don't act innocent," he growled, showing his teeth. "I've been onto you for quite some time."

"What do you mean, 'onto' me?" Nancy said.

"I spotted you following me out of the landfill," Slade snapped. "I'm a private eye, remember? Now, are you going to drop this business or aren't you?"

"It's too late," Nancy shot back. "Especially now that the police are involved again."

"Let me tell you something," he said, giving her a twisted little smile. "I don't believe for a minute that Christopher Johnson is still alive, but one thing I do believe—there's a whole lot of cash out there somewhere, just waiting for somebody to find it. And that somebody is going to be me, not some wet-behind-the-ears amateur detective. Got that?" He let go of her neck.

Nancy's mind was whirling. "Let me see if I understand you," she said. "All you care about is the cash?"

"That's right," Slade snapped.

"So if I nail Johnson, that's okay with you?"

"You can't nail a corpse—especially when it's in a million pieces." Slade laughed.

"Still," Nancy persisted. "If I do find him?"

"You can have him, for all I care," Slade said. "Just stay away from the money. If you don't, I'll take care of you. For good!" He reached for the door handle. "Remember that." After he got out, he slammed the car door.

Breathing heavily, Nancy hightailed it out of the parking garage. Back on the road, with Brewster growing smaller in her rearview mirror, her thoughts began to come together.

She went over and over Hal Slade's remarks. She had believed that Slade was Johnson's accomplice, but when Slade threatened her, he seemed genuinely convinced that Johnson was dead.

Slade would have been the perfect accomplice, but it seemed it wasn't Slade—so who could it be? Someone Mark had never even mentioned, maybe?

Suddenly Nancy thought of the dark-haired woman from the auction house. That story had all but slipped her mind until now. Maybe she should tell Mark about it, though. If there was a woman at Crabtree with long, dark hair, then maybe she was the one they were after.

Back in River Heights, she drove to the pizza place. Bess and George were waiting for Mark, and Nancy sat them all down and filled them in on her excursion.

"Slade! Hey," Mark said. "Do you think it was Slade who ransacked my apartment? I mean, now that we know he was the one who bought the desk and hired the thugs who broke it apart."

"Gee, Nancy," Bess said, "Do you think so?"

Nancy nodded slowly. "It makes sense. If he was looking for a clue to the missing cash in the desk, he didn't find it. Maybe he thought Mark had found it first."

"I didn't," Mark lamented.

"That's right," Nancy said. "But whoever ransacked your apartment didn't know that."

"Well, the money wasn't in the desk. Or Mark's apartment," Bess said.

"I'm not so sure it wasn't in the desk," Nancy said. She went on. "Remember, George, I told you how the auctioneer said a dark-haired woman had gotten there before us?"

"Right!" George gasped. "So you think that woman might have found it in the desk before the auction started and walked off with it?"

"That's what I'm thinking," Nancy replied. "I'm also thinking that the dark-haired woman might be Johnson's accomplice. Any ideas who it might be, Mark? Is there anyone at Crabtree who matches that description?"

Mark's brows came together, and his lips pursed. "Amanda George, maybe. She's one of the assistants Slade put on the case. But I don't know—Amanda doesn't seem like the criminal type."

"You never can tell, Mark," Nancy said. "Very sweet people have committed murder."

Suddenly she gasped. It had just occurred to her that there was one name they kept leaving out—one person who was in an excellent position to act as Johnson's accomplice. In fact, it was so obvious she couldn't believe she'd missed it.

"Linda Bates!" she said aloud.

"Linda?" Mark looked startled. "Don't be

crazy, Nancy! She'd never do that! Besides, she's blond, and we're looking for someone with brown hair."

Nancy sighed. Mark was so hopelessly in love with Linda that he'd never think anything bad about her. "A wig would change her hair color, Mark," she pointed out. "Let me put it this way. On occasion, you do confide in her, don't you?"

Mark was taken aback. "I—I suppose I do," he admitted. "But—Linda?"

Although Nancy didn't say anything to Mark, her newfound suspicions about Linda seemed more and more justified. For one thing, Linda's behavior toward Mark wasn't very consistent. When she'd talked to Nancy, she put Mark down and made it clear that she didn't want to see him.

But when Mark had refused to drop the Johnson case, Linda had arranged for him to stay with her aunts. And according to Mark, they talked on the phone all the time. Maybe she had asked the Bradford sisters to keep an eye on him as well.

"I'll tell you what I think," Nancy said to her friends. "I think Linda Bates and maybe her aunts, too, are in this up to their necks. We'd better have a chat with those nice little old ladies—right now."

The four of them piled into the car and soon Nancy was pulling up at the curb in front of the Bradford house. The sisters were not out on the porch. They climbed the steps to ring the bell to their ground floor flat.

"Hey, look at this!" said Bess, pointing to an envelope taped to Mark's front door. It said Mark Rubin on the front.

Mark tore it open and read the note out loud.

Dear Mark,

Please forgive us for leaving on such short notice. We didn't know until today that we were going abroad, but sometimes things happen fast! When your apartment was broken into we were upset. Linda must have seen how frightened we were, because this morning she came over with airline tickets for us! We're off to the South Pacific, can you believe it? We'll be back in two weeks. Please give the rent check to Linda. And could you water the geraniums? Thanks.

The letter was signed Frances Bradford.

Nancy was as startled as the others. "I guess Linda wanted her aunts out of the way so they couldn't answer any questions," she said.

Mark put the letter in his pocket and sighed deeply. His face registered his hurt. "I should have seen this coming. I guess I'm just not cut out to be a detective. Oh, well. I'll water the plants, at least." He disappeared inside his apartment.

Nancy shook her head and sat down in Frances Bradford's chair to think. Bess and George plopped down next to her on the glider.

George looked at Nancy. "Well?"

"Well," Nancy began, "Johnson always seems to be one step ahead of us, doesn't he?"

"So Linda must be his accomplice," Bess said.

"It sure makes all the pieces fit, doesn't it?" Nancy said. "Let's go over it—Johnson knows an investigation is about to start, so he plants Linda at Crabtree and then hires the agency to do the investigation. When Mark stumbles onto him, Johnson sets up his escape and fakes his own death."

Bess and George listened closely.

"Now," Nancy continued, "Johnson thinks he's safe—that is, until that crazy Mark Rubin keeps pursuing the case. Johnson has Linda set Mark up somewhere where they can keep an eye on him until he calms down. But he doesn't calm down. Worse, he spots Johnson downtown one day and brings Nancy Drew in on the case."

"So far so good," George said, nodding.

"What happens next?" Bess looked spellbound.

"Now it gets a little fuzzier," Nancy had to

admit. "But here goes: Johnson must be hanging around River Heights for a reason, otherwise he'd be out of the country already, right?"

Bess and George nodded.

Nancy went on, speaking slowly. "Maybe what was in the desk was something he needed —like a key to a safety deposit box. A safety deposit box filled with a million dollars. Johnson can't get the money out without the key."

"Why would he have left the key in his desk?" George asked.

"I don't know," Nancy said, shaking her head. "But for whatever reason, before he faked his death, he couldn't go back to his apartment to get it. And afterward the police had sealed it off."

"Hey, that makes sense!" Bess said, her eyes lighting up.

Nancy nodded. "The way I see it, the dark-haired woman—Linda in a wig—took the key out of the desk at the auction hall. That's why Slade didn't find it."

George frowned. "How did Slade know about the key? A lucky guess?" Nancy nodded.

"That would mean that Johnson and Linda have the key now," George pointed out. "So why haven't they left town?"

"I don't know," Nancy said. "If this whole theory is solid," she added, "then Johnson has had the key since the night of the auction."

Nancy massaged her eyes, trying to clear her mind. The three girls looked up as Mark shuffled back out onto the porch, a watering can in his hand. He silently started watering the flowers.

As Nancy watched, she remembered one of the Bradford sisters telling her that Linda had bought them the planter of flowers. Something about it was nibbling at her memory. Then it came to her.

She formed a mental picture of the moment she'd come downstairs with the Bradford sisters, the day Mark's rooms had been ransacked. Linda was in the house making tea. There'd been dirt on the porch floor, and Marie had lamented that she had spent all morning sweeping. . . .

Nancy snapped to attention. She jumped up. Pushing Mark aside, she bent over the flowers and dug her fingers into the wet soil.

"W-what?" Mark sputtered, standing aside.

George and Bess exchanged glances. "What are you doing?" George ventured.

"Give me a minute," Nancy said impatiently.

It didn't take her long to retrieve her prize—a plastic film canister containing a small key. There was a bank logo on it—the same bank Nancy had visited the other day. "The key to Johnson's safety deposit box!"

Nancy announced, holding it up for them all to see.

"Oh, boy," Mark murmured.

"This proves that Linda is Christopher Johnson's accomplice, Mark," Nancy said levelly. "I'm afraid there's no doubt about it now."

He nodded sadly.

"I don't get it, Nan," George said. "Why did she hide the key here?"

Nancy smiled. "Because Slade was looking for it. Maybe she was afraid he was onto her. And he'd already looked here when he tore Mark's apartment apart. He wasn't likely to come back and look again."

"But why haven't Linda and Johnson come for it yet?" Bess wondered.

Mark gave a little laugh. "Probably waiting for their passports to come in the mail. You know how slow the government is—"

Nancy gasped. "Mark! You're a genius!" she cried out.

Mark blinked. "I am?" he said.

Nancy patted his shoulder. "Yes, you are. Remember the forger? Artie Wilson?"

All three nodded their heads.

"This completes the picture. Johnson hired Wilson to forge new passports for him and Linda. But Wilson violated his parole and got thrown in jail before he could finish! That would explain why Linda and Johnson didn't leave town after they'd gotten the key. Linda hid it here to keep it safe till Wilson is released and can finish their fake passports. Then she and Johnson will come for the key, pick up the money, and vanish!"

"Nancy," Bess exclaimed. "When was that forger supposed to get out of jail, anyway?"

"Friday at five P.M.," she recalled. "Today!"

Bess shrieked. "It's three-thirty now!"

"Come on, Mark." Nancy slipped the key into her pocket and grabbed his arm. "We're going to meet Wilson at the prison gate. If we dog his footsteps he'll have to lead us to Johnson!"

"Hey, what about us?" Bess called after them. She and George stood waiting on the porch.

"Wait at George's," Nancy told them. "Four people tailing one guy is too many—we'd give ourselves away."

Getting into the car, Nancy and Mark sped off toward the jail.

"Wait here, Mark," Nancy instructed as they pulled up outside. "I'll find out where prisoners are released so we can get into position and tail Wilson." She went up to the desk and made a discreet inquiry about Artie Wilson.

"I'm sorry, miss," the clerk said. "When prisoners are due out on Friday afternoon we usually let them out early. Artie Wilson was gone at three o'clock. You just missed him."

Nancy stood still for a moment, too stunned to react. If Johnson, Linda, and Wilson had already met up, where would they go? To get the key to the safety deposit box at the Bradford house, of course!

Nancy ran back out to the car. "Come on!" she cried. "We can still catch them, but we haven't got a moment to lose!" She gunned the engine, and they drove back to George's house.

To her surprise, the cousins weren't there. Nancy and Mark looked at the Bradford sisters' house. Bess and George were not on the porch.

Nancy's heart was pounding. Something was wrong. Then she spotted the note, pinned to the door with a penknife.

Mark worked the knife free and read the note out loud.

"'We've got your friends. Do as we say and they won't get hurt.'"

"George and Bess!" Nancy said, putting her hands to her face. "They've been kidnapped!"

Chapter

Fifteen

Lᴇᴛ ᴍᴇ sᴇᴇ ᴛʜᴀᴛ," Nancy said, taking the note from Mark to read the rest of it. " 'Meet us at the landfill—nine tonight. Bring the key. No cops, no tricks, or your friends are history.' "

Nancy swallowed hard. "We blew it, Mark," she said. "We should never have left them here alone."

"This is my fault," Mark moaned. "I should never have dragged you into this case."

"No, it's not your fault," Nancy reassured him. "I should have seen this coming. They had to come back here to get the key."

"Hey, you didn't know Wilson was going to be let out early!" Mark grabbed Nancy by the shoulders. "Anyway, don't worry. We'll save them."

Before Nancy could stop him, Mark dashed upstairs. In a moment he was back down. Grinning at Nancy, he bent over, lifted his trouser leg, and revealed an ankle holster with a gun in it!

Nancy put her hands on her hips. "Are you out of your mind? What are you doing with a gun?"

"Don't you have one?" Mark asked, surprised.

"No way," Nancy answered. "As far as I'm concerned, guns cause more trouble than they're worth. Like right now, for instance. The letter says no tricks. Let's not give Johnson an excuse to hurt Bess and George."

"But they'll kill all of us, Nancy!" Mark protested. "We've got to be prepared."

"There are better ways to prepare than carrying a gun, Mark. Please leave it behind," Nancy told him. "Most times, guns wind up hurting the wrong people. I'm going to call Chief McGinnis and tell him what's going on. There's only one way out of that landfill. The police will nab Johnson—and Linda—after we meet with them."

Mark shook his head. "I still can't believe she's involved in this," he said. "I guess love really is blind, huh?"

"Sometimes," Nancy replied. "Just try to keep your eyes open tonight, when you and Linda come face-to-face. Remember, you're on opposite sides of the law now." With that, she went up to Mark's apartment and called police headquarters.

Chief McGinnis was glad to hear from Nancy. "I've left three messages at your home," he told her. "Where've you been?"

Nancy told the chief about Bess and George's kidnapping.

The chief gave a heavy sigh. "You'd better go ahead with the rendezvous," he told her.

"The note said 'no cops,'" Nancy warned.

"Don't worry. You won't see us, but we'll be there. In force," said the chief. "And, Nancy, be careful. Johnson is as dangerous as they come."

Several hours later as dusk fell over River Heights, Nancy and Mark headed out to the landfill. Nancy tried to brief her partner on how to handle himself.

"I've been in situations like this before," she explained matter-of-factly. "The main thing is, don't make them mad. Find out what they want, what their plan is, then stay alert for your moment. And remember, we don't have to overpower them ourselves. The police will be waiting for them. All we have to do is survive." Not necessarily an easy task, Nancy reminded herself.

Soon, the landfill loomed ahead of them, its steep slopes grass covered and eerie. The night was dark, with only dim light from the moon filtering down through windswept clouds.

"Should we leave your car here at the bottom of the hill and sneak up on them?" Mark asked. They had reached the spot where they'd hidden on the night of the auction, while the two men above had set fire to Johnson's desk.

"No way," Nancy said. "They know we're coming at nine. There's no way we could possibly get the jump on them."

"We should have gotten here earlier," Mark muttered.

"No, it's better this way," Nancy told him. "Let's not look for a fight. Please, Mark," she begged, seeing the reluctance on his face. "Don't screw this up by trying to be a hero."

Mark bit his lip. "Can't I at least watch for them to let down their guard?"

Nancy blew out a breath. "Just don't go off half-cocked, okay?" she said.

"Right." Mark stared into the darkness ahead of them. "Flashlights up ahead," he announced, as the car wound around the terraced hillside.

Nancy braked to a stop at the edge of the landfill. The hill sloped down steeply. A car was parked at the edge. In front of it stood a man Nancy guessed had to be Christopher Johnson. He held a flashlight in one hand, and a gun in the other.

"Welcome to my scenic rendezvous," he

said with a debonair gesture as they emerged from the car. "You'll find it has quite a view—and if you don't breathe, you can almost ignore the smell."

"It smells, all right," Mark retorted angrily. "Just like this scheme of yours."

"Cool it, Mark," Nancy whispered out of the side of her mouth. Johnson looked just as he had in the window of Artie Wilson's apartment. The mustache, she could see at this distance, was real, probably grown after the helicopter explosion. The flat cap sat on his head at a jaunty angle.

Glancing at Mark, she could see that his eyes were riveted on Johnson's gun. Johnson also caught Mark's gaze. "I wouldn't try anything rash," he advised. "My darling fiancée, Linda, is right behind you, and she has a very nasty weapon in her hands."

Sure enough, behind them and about fifty feet away stood Linda Bates, toting what looked like an Uzi submachine gun. At her feet were three people, all bound and gagged.

Wait a minute, thought Nancy. Three? Then she saw who was next to Bess and George—Hal Slade!

"Surprised, huh, Nancy? Well, Slade was getting too nosy," Linda called out. She gave a nasty laugh, then ambled nearer to Mark.

"So you were engaged to Johnson this whole time?" he asked, sounding outraged.

"Poor baby," she said, pouting a little. "I'm sorry I had to deceive you. You're handsome when you're angry, though."

To his credit, Mark held his tongue, but there was fury and betrayal in his eyes.

"Did you bring the key?" Johnson asked Nancy, all business.

Nancy reached into her pocket and brought it out. "Is this the one you had in mind?" she asked, holding it up for them to see.

"You're a very good detective, young lady," Johnson told her. "Linda and I both thought there could be nothing safer than stashing the key at the Bradfords'. You proved us wrong. Now toss it over."

Nancy did as she was told. Glittering in the silver moonlight, it fell to the ground and Johnson picked it up. "Thanks," he said cheerfully.

"Now what?" Nancy asked, glancing at the three bound bodies and trying not to sound as nervous as she felt. Bess and George were staying as still as they could, and the police were probably moving into position. If she could just stall Johnson and Linda for another five minutes.

Johnson walked closer, with Linda at his side. "Now we tie you and this young man up, just like your friends, and drive you back to the Bradford house. There, you remain until somebody finds you. By then, we'll be safely out of the country with the brand-new passports Artie Wilson is making for us tonight. The bank opens at nine—how considerate of them to be open on Saturdays—and our flight leaves at ten-thirty. Now if you'll both turn around—"

He picked a coil of rope off the ground and approached Nancy.

Nancy caught a movement out of the corner of her eye and glanced sideways at Mark. His hands were at his sides, and he was clenching his fists. There was a wild, glazed look in his eyes.

Mark, no! she thought.

As Johnson approached, Mark leaped at him, knocking him backward onto the ground. Mark, still standing, reached for his pants leg.

Nancy gasped in horror. Mark had brought the gun! Glancing behind her, Nancy saw Linda running toward them.

"Mark, you're covered!" Nancy screamed.

Mark wasn't listening. He was tripping all over himself. The gun was stuck in its holster. Mark fell to the ground with a thud, just as Linda was about to hit him with her Uzi. She pointed the muzzle at his nose. Johnson moved forward and quickly disarmed him.

"Nancy, why didn't you help me?" Mark demanded.

"Because I don't want to die!" she shot back furiously.

"Unfortunately," Johnson said, "that's just what's going to happen now that you've broken our terms. Obviously I cannot count on you to cooperate. Cover me, Linda."

Johnson went about his task with a vengeance, tying both Mark and Nancy so tightly that it hurt them just to breathe. Johnson and Linda dragged their five prisoners to Nancy's Mustang, crowding them all inside.

Nancy was in the driver's seat, with Bess's feet in her face. George was splayed across the back seat, Mark's legs were sticking up over the back seat, and Slade, in an impossibly contorted position, stared at Nancy from the passenger seat. All had been gagged as well as bound.

Johnson closed the car doors. Reaching in through the open driver's window, he started the engine. "Bon voyage, all of you," he said, putting the car into Drive and releasing the parking brake.

Nancy felt the Mustang roll forward, and she knew it was heading straight toward the edge of the hill. If they went over, they didn't have a chance!

Chapter

Sixteen

NANCY COULDN'T BREATHE. The blood roared furiously in her ears, and her eyes were riveted to the spot about a hundred feet away, where the hill dropped sharply off into the darkness of the garbage-filled dump. It was going to be a long, frightening, deadly trip down.

The other passengers squirmed in terror, frantically trying to work free of the ropes that bound them. Something rose up in Nancy—a stubborn, absolute refusal to die. She looked down at the Mustang's automatic gearshift, on the floor between her and Slade, and struggled with the ropes that held her wrists.

The car kept rolling at a slow, steady pace, gradually picking up speed. Any second now, it would go over the edge, and there would be nothing Nancy or anybody else could do.

Nancy twisted down into the seat. It was a painful, contorted position, but her head was only inches from the gearshift. Summoning up all her strength and twisting against the ropes, she banged the side of it with the top of her head, pushing the button that freed the shift. At the same time, she tried to push the shift back one notch.

With a terrible screech of the automatic transmission, the Mustang threw itself into reverse. Nancy was hurled against the dashboard.

The car was on the very edge, and no ground was visible in front of them. The fatal drop yawned below, but the car pulled back from the edge, driving in a crazy circle, then another, round and round.

Nancy was sure her last effort had been useless, that they would end up going over anyway, when suddenly the Mustang rammed into a parked bulldozer with a sickening crash. The car stopped moving. The engine sputtered and died.

Then—silence. They were safe!

Nancy looked around her. Bess and George were stirring in the back seat. They seemed to be all right. But Mark and Hal Slade looked unconscious, probably from the jolt when the car crashed against the bulldozer.

Nancy hoped they weren't seriously hurt, but there was nothing she could do right then, bound and gagged as she was. If only the police would arrive!

Sirens answered Nancy's silent plea. The sounds came nearer and nearer. Soon, Chief McGinnis's worried face poked through the window. Nancy had never been happier to see him.

"Well, now, what do we have here?" the chief said jovially. He opened the door and started freeing Nancy and the others.

"Did you get them, Chief?" Nancy asked as soon as the gag was removed from her mouth.

"Johnson and the girl? We got them, all right." McGinnis beamed. "Sorry we weren't here sooner, but there was an accident on the road. We got Wilson, too—the old guy is back behind bars, and this time I don't think he'll be out for a while. Thanks, Nancy. We couldn't have done it without you."

Nancy blushed and changed the subject. "Better call a doctor," she told him. "The two guys are out cold."

Chief McGinnis radioed in the call for help, then reached over and checked Mark's and Slade's pulses. "They'll be all right," he assured the girls. "No blood anywhere, and they're breathing. They probably have concussions."

Nancy shook her head and threw the chief a

weary smile. "Now, why is it always the men who faint when the going gets tough?"

YOUNG DETECTIVE SOLVES
BIZARRE CASE OF LIVING DEAD!

A *Today's Times* Exclusive
by Brenda Carlton

River Heights has a new star detective. He's golden-haired, blue-eyed, twenty-two-year-old Mark Rubin, and he's just cracked the biggest case of his career.

Last night at the town landfill, Rubin cleverly trapped criminal Christopher Johnson and his accomplice, Linda Bates, who had kidnapped two local teenage girls. Rubin was able to turn the tables on the crooks, who fled into the waiting arms of the River Heights police.

According to River Heights's own Nancy Drew, who also played a role in the dramatic events, Johnson, an embezzler, had been presumed dead. . . .

Nancy put the newspaper down and stopped reading. George and Bess looked at her from across the Drews' living room with annoyed expressions.

"Ooh, that Brenda Carlton! She makes it sound as if you hardly had anything to do with capturing Johnson!" Bess seethed. "What's wrong with that girl, anyway?"

"I think she looked into Mark's deep blue eyes and was swept away," George joked. "Anyway, Bess," she added, "I was there when Nancy gave Brenda the story. Nancy did give Mark most of the credit."

"But it was you who solved it, Nan," Bess protested.

Settling into her dad's brown leather chair, Nancy smiled. "I figured Mark needed the boost," she explained. "I thought it might help his battered ego."

"I guess so," Bess said, nodding in agreement. "If Mark was my boyfriend, I'd make sure he never had ego problems."

"What's this? Are you getting ideas, Bess?" George teased.

"Well, he is free now, isn't he?" Bess challenged.

"Yes, but I wouldn't say he's much of a prize—despite his looks," George counseled her cousin.

Bess arched an eyebrow provocatively. "Are you sure you're not just saying that because you've got an eye on him yourself?"

Nancy shook her head, amused. Thank goodness she had Ned Nickerson. And now that the case was over, she was going to visit him at Emerson College as soon as she could.

"Anyway, Nancy, I still don't see why you

told Brenda it was all Mark's doing," George said. "No matter what you say, Mark knows you were the one who did everything."

"Come on, I didn't do everything," Nancy corrected her. "Mark was the one who brought me in on this case, remember. If it wasn't for his persistence, I wouldn't even have stayed involved. He made some very good deductions, too," she added.

"But don't forget he almost got us all killed, trying to pull that gun of his," George added.

Nancy nodded. "That was dumb of him," she agreed. "I hope he's learned his lesson."

"Come to think of it, I guess he is a little too intense for me," Bess said.

The phone rang, interrupting her. Nancy picked it up. "Hello?"

"Nancy? It's me, Mark!" came the excited voice on the other end of the line.

"Mark, hi! Are your ears burning? We were just talking about you," Nancy said.

"Did you see the paper? Isn't it fantastic!" Mark sounded more enthusiastic than ever.

"Gee, Mark, it's just an article," Nancy started to say.

"Just an article?" Mark replied. "Well, guess who read it? Archer Crabtree, that's who. He just called me with a job offer!"

"Mark, that's great!" Nancy cried. "Bess, George, Mark got his old job back!"

Mark interrupted her. "Not my old job,

Nancy—a new job. He made me a full detective! I'm taking over Hal Slade's position! Well, not exactly his position, since he had a lot of seniority. I'm already on another case, can you believe it! And, Nancy, this is a really big one—next time you see my face it's going to be on the cover of the Chicago *Times!*"

He launched into a description of his new case, which had something to do with a military contractor defrauding the government. By the time she hung up the phone, Nancy's mind was reeling.

She told Bess and George all his news, then made a face. "I hope I haven't created a monster!" she confessed.

The three girls broke into gales of laughter. "Oh, well," Nancy managed to say at last. "From now on, when Mark has a problem, it's his, not mine."

"Don't be too sure of that, Nancy," George teased her. "What do you want to bet that the first time he runs into trouble, Mark will be back on your doorstep."

"Yeah," Bess chimed in. "Mark Rubin may be an up-and-comer as a detective, but he's got a long way to go before he's as good as the one and only Nancy Drew!"

Nancy's next case:

While vacationing in the U.S. Virgin Islands, Nancy, Bess, and George learn that one of the hottest rock groups around is filming a music video at their resort. But something sinister is brewing beneath the palm trees, turning the island retreat into a danger zone.

Band member Ricky Angeles has twice been the victim of attempted murder but refuses to tell Nancy why. She suspects that the resort is a front for a criminal enterprise, and that Ricky's the one with the most to lose. The shocking truth may compel him—and Nancy—to face the worst kind of music . . . in *HOT PURSUIT*, Case #58 in The Nancy Drew Files™.